RAMBO

FIRST BLOOD PART II

MARIO KASSAR and ANDREW VAJNA present
SYLVESTER STALLONE
RAMBO/FIRST BLOOD PART II
RICHARD CRENNA
Music by JERRY GOLDSMITH
Produced by BUZZ FEITSHANS
Directed by GEORGE P. COSMATOS
Screenplay by SYLVESTER STALLONE and JAMES CAMERON
Story by KEVIN JARRE
Based on characters created by DAVID MORRELL
Filmed in PANAVISION®

RAMBO

FIRST BLOOD PART II

The novel by David Morrell

From the screenplay by Sylvester Stallone and James Cameron

A JOVE BOOK

RAMBO FIRST BLOOD PART II

A Jove Book / published by arrangement with
the author and Anabasis Investments, N.V.

PRINTING HISTORY
Jove edition / May 1985

ISBN: 0-515-08399-2

Jove books are published by The Berkley Publishing Group,
200 Madison Avenue, New York, N.Y. 10016.
The words "A JOVE BOOK" and the "J" with sunburst
are trademarks belonging to Jove Publications, Inc.

PRINTED IN THE UNITED STATES OF AMERICA

To Stirling Silliphant,
for October 7, 1960, and the first episode of "Route 66,"
for teaching me to love a story

To Tiana Alexandra-Silliphant,
who lived there and survived

Contents

Author's Note

In my novel *First Blood,* Rambo died. In the films, he lives.

Thanks to Andrew Vajna, Mario Kassar, and Robert Brenner at Carolco productions (and a special nod to Jeanne Joe) for expediting my research on this project.

To Dara Marks at the Westgate Group . . .

To Sylvester Stallone and James Cameron, also thanks.

The weapons described in this book (and used in the film *Rambo)* exist. They are functional. More, they are works of art.

The knife was created by Jimmy Lile, "the Arkansas Knifesmith," Route 1, Russellville, Arkansas 72801. Mr. Lile also made the now famous knife that was used in the movie *First Blood.* The present knife is somewhat different, though equally dramatic. As with the *First Blood* knife, one hundred marked and serial-numbered *Rambo* copies have been sold to collectors. An unnumbered slightly different version of both knives is available to the public. A six-inch *Rambo* throwing knife is also available.

The bow was created by Hoyt/Easton Archery, 7800 Haskell Ave., Van Nuys, California 91406. It, too, is available. Thanks to Joe Johnston for teaching me about its intricacy. Kathy Velardi supplied me with helpful information. Bob Rhode answered my questions about the history of archery.

The arrows were developed by Pony Express Sport Shop, 16606 Schoenborn St., Sepulveda, California 91343. Thanks to Joe Ellithorpe for explaining their unique capabilities.

– I –

THE QUARRY

— 1 —

With profound contentment, immersed in the purity of a perfect timeless Zen moment, Rambo swung the heavy sledgehammer up from behind him. He ignored its weight, however, and instead enjoyed its satisfying arc as it passed the zenith above his shoulder. Pushing the total force of his spirit behind his thrust, he walloped the hammer down as hard as he could upon the iron wedge sunk into the fascinating, beautiful (because it existed) white rock. Every crag and pock mark on its overwhelming surface magnified before his gaze. And with the ringing impact of metal on metal, the rock disintegrated, fragments exploding like shrapnel, the wedge at last falling . . .

Free. As the word occurred to him, he stiffened, thrusting it from his mind.

No.

He shook his head.

He mustn't think of being free.

He mustn't think at all.

Just do.

A drop of sweat, one of many oozing from his forehead, broke loose, glinting as it fell, disintegrating upon the wedge, exploding as the stone had. Its sunlight-reflecting fragments reminded him again . . .

Of shrapnel. Rockets from gun ships. Booby traps. Claymore mines. Grenades. The jungle erupting. Soldiers screaming. Blood . . .

Don't think.

If you want to survive, just do.

He jammed the wedge into another rock, raised the hammer again, and swung it down with fierce concentration.

Again!

And again!

And . . . !

Around him, the same heavy ear-piercing clang of metal striking metal echoed through the wide deep quarry. Heat waves shimmered off the sun-baked rocks. Men in tattered prison work clothes, their sweat-stained tanktops stenciled with P on the back, raised sledgehammers of their own, inhaling, listing from exhaustion, and again . . . and again! struck a metal wedge to rupture a rock.

But they didn't know the secret, Rambo thought. They grumbled at night, pissed and moaned about their fate, complained about their hardship.

They didn't know that nothing mattered. Nothing.

Except survival.

Existence itself.

Even pain could be wonderful. If you put your mind in the right perspective. If you shut out the past and future and forced yourself to concentrate on the vividness of the present, even if now was filled with pain.

His muscles aching, he glanced toward the square-faced sullen guards who studied every movement of every prisoner, carefully, from a distance, holding twelve-gauge shotguns or .30/06 Springfield rifles equipped with telescopic sights.

Don't let the bastards get you down.

Sometimes, when he swung his hammer, feeling his taut bulging muscles absorb the impact against the wedge, he thought back to the violence that had brought him here. The town. The cop. Yes, Teasle. Why wouldn't that son-of-a-bitch back off?

A corner of his mind replied, *And why wouldn't you?*

I had a right.

To do?

What I wanted in the country I sacrificed my soul to fight for.

4

You have to admit you looked strange to him.

Because I'd been sleeping in the woods? Because I hadn't shaved and needed a haircut? I wasn't hurting anybody. He didn't have a reason to roust me.

But you could have explained. You have to admit you looked like a vagrant. Admit it. You didn't have a job.

Doing what? Who'd hire me? There's only one thing I was trained for. In Nam, they trusted me with million-dollar equipment. I flew a gunship. Over here, I can't get a job parking cars. Jesus!

He struck his hammer against the wedge in fury.

Teasle. He kept pushing me. Arrested me. Told his men to shave me. Like that bastard North Vietnamese who took his knife to me and gave me these souvenirs on my chest and back.

So you lost control.

No. Defended myself!

Broke from jail and played hell with that posse in the mountains. They didn't have a chance. You shot up—blew away—that town. And think of what you did to that cop. And now . . .

Rambo nodded, seething. His Zen moment totally destroyed, he raised the sledge in blinding rage, determined to destroy, annihilate, another rock.

And now he was paying for the war he'd fought. Oh, sure, they trained me. They were pleased as hell to send me over there.

But why did they figure I'd just forget? Why didn't they take as much trouble detraining me?

Or maybe that isn't possible. Maybe you just don't belong.

After six months in a North Vietnam prison camp? Don't belong? You'd better believe it. After that, the only place you think you belong is in hell.

Like now. One prison replaced by another.

But this time in America. The home of the brave. The land of the free.

If only that cop had . . .

5

What?

Just asked me how I was doing.

— 2 —

He set down his hammer and wiped his muscular forearm across his brow, though that gesture wasn't any help—both his arm and brow were equally drenched with sweat. He glanced at the nearest guard, then toward the water bucket on a shelf of rock ten feet up the slope.

The guard responded to his upraised eyebrows by nodding slightly, stern-lipped.

Rambo trudged up the path. A thin black convict was there ahead of him. *Too* thin, Rambo thought, watching him drink from the ladle attached to the bucket. Their eyes met briefly.

Shit, I don't think I can stand this, the black man seemed to say.

Keep thinking that way and you won't, a part of Rambo's mind decided. But all he allowed his eyes to say was, Yeah, it's tough, all right. Hang loose.

The black man nodded, descending wearily to his spot in the quarry.

Rambo dipped the ladle into the dust-filmed water, drinking. It tasted rusty and hot. But in Nam he'd tasted worse, he decided, and poured a ladleful over his back. It didn't cool him.

"Rambo!" a gruff voice commanded.

Turning sharply, he faced two guards, their features and

bodies almost indistinguishable in the blinding sun behind their heads.

He didn't speak. To do so was, of course, forbidden. If he did, he risked reprisal, the jab of a rifle butt, the wallop of a club.

"*This* way," the gruff voice said—the guard on the left, pointing up the slope. "Walk ahead of us." They held their weapons ready.

Rambo forced himself to show no reaction.

But his stomach contracted, curiosity mixing with suspicion, as he did what he was told.

His misgivings intensified when he heard the guard behind growl, "Yeah, whatever the Christ is going on, they told me to bring you, pal. A command appearance, you might say. From the top. You've got a visitor."

— 3 —

His name was Trautman, Samuel. Colonel. Special Forces. U.S. Army. A tall, lean, ferret-faced man in colorful full-dress uniform, his Green Beret worn proudly. Of his fifty years, almost half had been spent in the military. He'd learned (and later taught) how to kill with every weapon from an AK-47 to a ballpoint pen. He'd fought in jungles, deserts, and mountain ranges, watched men whom he'd thought of as sons blown apart, their bloody fragments pelting him, been wounded three times . . .

But what he did now made all of that insignificant. Everything else had been like boot camp. He faced the hardest task of his career.

His thick-soled military boots echoed harshly down the corridor. Metal doors with small barred openings lined each side. Overhead lights glared, making him squint. He smelled sweat, stale air, and something else, deeper, more nostril-flaring, the stench of desperation.

Despair.

Flanked by a guard, he reached the end. ". . . This one?" He nodded toward the final door.

"You'd better step back." The guard drew a .45 pistol, tugged a ring of keys from a clip on his belt, and fitted one into the lock. It turned with a scrape. "I'll stand in the corner and make sure nothing happens."

"No."

The guard sighed. "Look, I know what my orders are. To let you talk to him alone. But this guy isn't. . .Let's put it this way. There are convicts, and there are convicts. This guy's as dangerous as they get. And I'm responsible for *him*, for *you*. He might take a notion to—"

"No."

The guard shook his head. "Okay, but you can't say I didn't warn you. If you're that determined, here, you'd better take this." He offered the pistol. "In case he—"

"Give me a break."

Trautman passed the guard and shoved at the unlocked door. It squeaked on its hinges, revealing a shadowy cramped compartment.

The guard flicked the light switch outside. It didn't work. "Sure. I might have figured."

"What?"

"Thinks he's the fucking Prince of Darkness."

Trautman ignored him. Stepping in—"Be careful," the guard said—he reached for the light bulb in the ceiling, turning it till it illuminated.

He glanced around. Concrete walls. A metal bunk bed bolted to the floor. A three-inch circular opening that served as a toilet in one corner in the floor. A tiny barred window directly across, too high to peer out of. Not that the view would have mattered—an adjacent wall shut out the sun.

He continued turning.

And in the corner to his left, crouched on his haunches as if at rest or about to spring, his eyes fierce, muscles tensed—

Was Rambo.

Jesus! Trautman thought. He remembered a panther that he'd once seen caged. It had paced for days, back and forth, back and forth, finally stopping, crouching, its eyes like black suns, waiting.

Frowning again at the narrow compartment, Trautman suddenly understood how Rambo must have felt when the walls started shrinking toward him in the basement of that police station where all of this had started.

No, that's wrong, Trautman thought. It started long before then.

But he understood something else, a sickening wave of pity—sorrow? grief?—sweeping over him. This was going to be a whole lot harder than he'd imagined.

"At ease." Trautman turned to shut the door, catching a glimpse of the apprehensive guard just before the barrier was shut and metal banged against metal, echoing off the walls.

"I'll wait," the guard said outside, his voice coming through the barred face-high opening.

"No, what you'll do is follow your orders," Trautman said. "You'll walk down that corridor. Leave us alone."

"I have to lock the door."

"Then what are you waiting for?"

The key scraped in the door. Trautman listened to the footsteps receding hollowly down the hallway and shifted his gaze toward Rambo, who hadn't moved, though Trautman had made a point of showing his back, a signal, a gesture of trust, of reassurance.

"At ease?" Trautman made it a question this time.

The compartment became terribly still.

Slowly, his muscles like springs unwinding under pressure, careful lest they suddenly snap into motion, Rambo stood.

The silence lengthened.

"John."

"Colonel." Rambo's eyes narrowed, searing.

Well, he was never much for small talk, Trautman thought. And maybe I'm not, either. ". . . You mind if I sit down?"

Squinting, Rambo might have nodded—it was hard to tell.

Trautman eased down onto the bunk. Its blanket felt scratchy, its mattress thin. The springs creaked. "Well . . . so this is home, huh?" He hoped it sounded like a joke.

It didn't.

Rambo squinted harder, shaking his head. "Out there. In the quarry. In the open. Maybe. Home? I don't know what . . . In here. These walls. They . . ."

"Hey, I know, John. Relax. I'm here to try to help. For what it's worth, I did everything I could to keep you from being sent to this hellhole."

Rambo bristled. "I've seen worse."

"Yes, you have . . ."—Trautman imagined the prison camp in North Vietnam where Rambo had been tortured— ". . . haven't you?" He peered down, distressed, noticing an object under the bed.

A battered shoebox. It surprised him. Nothing else in the cell seemed personal.

"May I?"

Rambo didn't answer.

Taking a chance, assuming he had permission, Trautman pulled out the shoebox.

But when he opened it and saw the contents, he had trouble speaking. ". . . This your stuff?"

"That's it."

Trautman swallowed sickly and sorted through.

Wrinkled ghostly snapshots. The men from Rambo's Special Forces unit. Individuals or in groups. Horsing around, sometimes not. In and out of uniform.

But one in particular made Trautman stare.

Rambo—younger, clean-shaven. Innocent. Grinning broadly.

Distressed, Trautman peered up toward the savaged man who stood across from him, the man who more than anyone he'd trained had been like his son. He cleared his throat and tried to sound casual. "Hardcore outfit. Best I ever worked with."

"Those men are all dead."

"But you're not."

"I might as well be."

Avoiding Rambo's blazing eyes, Trautman glanced again at the box. His throat felt swollen. "The Congressional Medal of Honor."

"Oh, yeah, the big time. That and a quarter'll get you a cup of coffee out there."

"Plus...?" But it didn't get any easier. "Two Silver Stars, four Bronze Stars, two Soldier's Crosses, four Vietnamese Crosses of Gallantry, and"—Trautman swallowed painfully—"a handful of Purple Hearts."

"Five. They let me keep that stuff. I never asked for it. I never wanted it."

"What *did* you want?"

"Wanted? I just...I don't know...after all that...I guess I just wanted one person, *one* person, to come up to me and shake my hand and say, 'You did good, John.' And mean it. Really mean it...after all that."

"You picked the wrong war to be a hero in."

"I didn't pick anything. And I never asked to be a so-called hero. All I did was..."

Trautman waited. "What you were trained to do."

"What someone else *asked* me to do. And what I was forced to do...to stay alive." He gestured toward the walls. "Alive."

The cell seemed to shrink. Trautman couldn't put it off any longer. "John, I..."—standing, he took a step forward—"...I promised I'd help you if I could."

Rambo stared.

"To get you out of here."

No reaction.

You interested?"

No answer.

"You can't possibly want to stay in here."

"But what do I have to do to get out? In here, at least I know where I stand. I hate these walls. But when I'm in the quarry, in the sun, in the open, it's not so bad. You might even say it's peaceful."

"Just hear me out first." Trautman shook his head. "No, that's wrong. Hear *both* of us."

"Both?"

"Let's take a walk."

Trautman banged on the door. "Out there, I know you're listening! Open this damned thing up!"

— 4 —

As if he faced a mirage, Rambo stared in wonderment at the lush wide lawn in front of the prison. Sprinklers watered it. They smelled like rain. Inhaling their sweetness, flanked by Trautman, he crossed a knoll, approaching a heavy man in a gray conservative suit.

Behind, two guards watched at a distance. He'd heard them snick their rifle bolts. The cuffs on his wrists had been shut extra tight.

They reached the man.

"This is Murdock," Trautman said. "And Murdock, Rambo."

Murdock extended his hand.

All Rambo could do was lift his wrists, showing the cuffs.

And Murdock grinned, then lit a cigarette. "Yeah, I see how they'd inconvenience you. Anyway, hello. It's good to meet you."

Rambo studied his face. There was something about the nondescript features, the cold glint in the eyes despite the heartless varsity smile. He glanced, troubled, at Trautman, then back at Murdock. "You a spook?"

Murdock lost his smile. He squinted. "Yeah, they told me you were quick on the uptake. That's right. I'm CIA. Special Operations Division."

"I don't work with spooks."

"We're not so bad. Once you get to know us."

"That's the trouble. I did. In Nam. In '68."

Approached by the CIA, an A-Team of Green Berets had been led to believe that they were under orders to assassinate a group of Viet Cong sympathizers in a village outside Saigon. When the mission was accomplished, it turned out that Intelligence had been mistaken, that the villagers who'd been shot were not Viet Cong—quite the opposite—and that Intelligence denied all knowledge of the operation. The A-Team was brought up on charges, convicted, and jailed in Saigon prior to being transported back to the States. Other Green Berets became so incensed that they planned an attack on the jail to rescue their combat-brothers, and when word of the plan was picked up by the CIA, the military command in Saigon began a systematic deemphasis of Special Forces missions, gradually reducing their strength in Southeast Asia, threatening to disassemble the unit.

Rambo hadn't been involved in the operation, but he'd known men who were, and he had no use for deceit.

"Sixty-eight?" Murdock asked. "Hey, an honest misunderstanding. Ancient history. And besides, you're missing the point." His eyes glinted colder. "Right now is what we're talking about. In case the good colonel here didn't tell you, I'm authorized to get you out of this place. I assumed that's what you wanted. Unless you get your jollies crushing rocks."

Rambo glanced past Murdock toward the sprinklers drenching the lawn. He remembered the quarry, the narrowing walls of his cell. As cool beads of moisture drifted over, settling on his chin, he stiffened. *If you want to survive, just do.* "It doesn't hurt to listen. What's the job?"

"Now, there you're talking. That's the attitude. The job? It's right up your alley. Classic Special Forces op . . . Hit fast . . . In and out. Two days."

"The army's got a lot of Green Berets. They're not in prison. Why come to me?"

"Why? Because we *like* you. Or at least the computer at Langley likes you. Popped up your file on the screen in seven seconds. Various factors. Service record. Area familiarity."

"Area?" Rambo frowned. "Where?"

"Not just yet. You haven't agreed."

"I won't jump blind."

"Hey, maybe I misunderstood." Murdock glared at Trautman. "I thought your boy wanted . . . It's yes or no. In or out . . . *Now.* If it's 'out,' we will *not* have had this conversation. If you come in, you will *not* be working for us. No knowledge. No comment. Do you read me?"

Murdock, who hadn't taken one puff from his cigarette, threw it on the lawn and crushed it with his wingtip shoe.

The sprinklers flitted in the background.

"Tell him," Trautman told Murdock, his voice harsh. "I'll take the responsibility."

"North Vietnam." Murdock pursed his lips in contempt. "What they call the Democratic Republic of Vietnam now."

Rambo tensed. He remembered the soldier whose knife had left the crisscross of scars on his chest and back. He remembered the pit into which he'd been lowered and the filth that the enemy soldiers had dumped down onto him. The wormy food? He'd eaten it. The excrement? He'd gotten used to it. And the scars? There wasn't a day—or a night— when he didn't want to get even for . . .

Trautman stepped ahead, and Rambo felt the warrior bond between them.

"John, what this is all about . . . We left some people behind there. POWs."

"You're telling me this has just occurred to somebody *now?*"

"We don't leave our men," Murdock said.

It felt wrong.

Yet right.

He stared at Trautman, seeing the commitment in Trautman's eyes, the hope, the need to win, Jesus, part, at least, of the war that they'd sacrificed their souls for.

"Okay, you've got it. I'm in."

With a flick of his wrist, he tossed the handcuffs onto the ground.

Murdock stared at them.

— 5 —

Alone, in the narrow cell, his knees crossed, sitting on the bone-chilling concrete floor, casting the shadow of a Buddha, Rambo stared toward the tiny circular opening below him that was his toilet.

Behind, at his unlocked door, he sensed the glowering presence of his frustrated impotent guard.

With religious deliberation, he opened his shoebox, staring at his possessions. His scraps of memory. The vestiges of long-departed friends.

Symbols of valor.

And of violent death.

He reached toward the heel of his shoe, as if by magic holding up a book of matches. He didn't need to look to know that the guard at the door jerked upright, his spine rigid, nervous.

Sure, that's right. Anytime I wanted to, I could have burned this place to the ground. I bet you wonder what else I've got hidden.

Holding the matches in one hand, he used the other to drop his medals one by one down the hole in the floor.

He heard an echoing distant splash.

Another.

Then another.

Another.

He didn't understand his motive, but it gave him a peculiar satisfaction. And he had a bad feeling about what awaited him. If he didn't come back, he didn't want anybody fooling with his stuff.

He opened the matchbook, detached one, struck it. The phosphorus gleamed.

And one by one, he touched his photographs to it. This friend. That friend. Each cascaded blazing toward the pit, extinguished hissing, echoing, somewhere below him.

And finally . . .

Himself.

Because his premonition kept growing. A sixth sense warning him that, when you dealt with Murdock, even the quarry could be better than . . .

He watched his former self, flaming, disintegrate.

But still not satisfied, he even torched the shoebox.

– 2 –

THE WOLF DEN

— 1 —

Bragg hadn't changed—that was something to take comfort from. The barracks, the mess hall, the armory, the infirmary, the motor pool, the parade ground and obstacle course and jump towers, all crowded with soldiers who, having distinguished themselves in conventional training, had arrived here to try to become elite. From a window in this room— Airborne Special Forces Group, Operations Center—he watched a platoon of first-week hopefuls clomping past in rhythmic lockstep.

A glaring sergeant matched his step to theirs, bellowing, "Three-fo-lef, lef-right...! Other lef, shithead! Square those shoulders! Keep those pieces straight, girls! I said keep 'em straight! Didn't they teach you pussies anything at...?"

The platoon disappeared from Rambo's sight. Years ago, in his innocence, he'd been one of them. Swallowing, he remembered his patriotism. His pride.

But if he'd known the consequences, he wondered, would he still have gone through the training?

Troubled, he studied the briefing room—an austere cubicle with the army's typically drab metal chairs and table. The overhead lights were harsh. A surveillance camera stared down at the group. Outside, two MPs guarded the door.

An aide came around the table and gave Rambo a sealed folder, then extended a clipboard and pen.

Across from Rambo, Murdock leaned forward. "This is your mission packet."

"Sign here, please," the aide said.

Rambo did.

"And here."

Rambo signed again.

"You can open it now," Murdock said. "Memorize the contents while you're here. Those documents do not leave this room."

Rambo broke the seal. From the packet, he removed a sheaf of photocopied documents.

Murdock leaned farther forward. "The twenty-four hundred American servicemen missing in action in Vietnam, Laos, and Cambodia are officially listed 'Presumed Killed.' Certainly most of them are."

Rambo leafed through the documents. Skipping a stack of imposing densely typed reports, he fished out several grainy eight-by-ten black-and-white photographs.

Murdock kept talking. "All the same, reports kept filtering in. Hearsay, mostly. Rumors. But then we got sightings by refugees or local sympathizers. Nothing verified, mind you. So many of them, though. And each year, they kept growing. More than twenty-three hundred sightings by now. Finally we have to get off the dime. To the League of Families, to Congress and a lot of Americans, this is still a very emotional issue. We think we've got enough to proceed on."

Rambo stared at the photographs. They'd been taken from an extremely high altitude, revealing a small compound of buildings, mostly huts, surrounded by dense vegetation, obscured by heat haze, in an eerie depression in the rain forest. For a moment, he didn't make the connection.

Then, with a sudden shock, he did.

But before he could speak, Murdock gestured toward the documents. "Memo E-7 will cover the details. An abandoned Vietnamese Army base in the north-central highlands may have a compound that's used as an internment camp. As you can see, the intelligence is soft. These LANDSAT photos show huts . . . barracks. It could be anything."

Rambo glared up from the photographs. His pulse sped,

pounding. "What the Christ are you trying to . . . ?"

Murdock straightened, his face flushed, indignant. *"Trying to what?"*

"You think I don't recognize this place? You think I went blind in that hole? You think I got suddenly stupid? This place is . . . !" His voice was so hoarse with rage that he couldn't finish.

But the unsaid words seemed to fill the room.

Murdock squinted, then turned to Trautman. "You called it."

"Of course. I told you."

"So you trained him, Colonel. You deal with it."

Murdock leaned back in his chair and folded his arms. "This mission's dicey enough without . . ."

Trautman caught Rambo's gaze and shrugged. "See, they figured you'd be grateful for the chance to quit breaking rocks. A logical assumption. No problem. And they figured your sense of loyalty would tempt you to want to get those fellow soldiers back. But what they *didn't* know was whether your experience in that prison camp . . . Yes, it's the same one you were held in." Trautman pursed his lips. "And were tortured in. Jesus! See, they didn't know if you'd react in the opposite way and tell them, 'Hell, no, what kind of damned fool do you think I am? I won't go back there.'"

Rambo controlled his breathing, trying to subdue his anger. "Spooks. They never change. There's always got to be one more lie."

"No." Murdock dropped his pen on the table. "Not lies. Restricted information. Need to know. I never lied to you. I just didn't tell you everything."

Rambo kept staring.

"All right," Murdock said. "You want to hear it all. Yes, that's the prison camp you escaped from. That's the target area. I told you the computer flashed your file on the screen in seven seconds. Because of your medals? Sure. Because you're a hardass? Naturally. Because you were once a POW yourself? Of course. But the point is, no one—I mean *no one*—understands that terrain better than you. Let's face it. The risk factor on this assignment is maximum. Who could figure what extra element might tip the balance and make you back off? But if you stick . . . if you go all the way . . . you'll be temporarily reinstated in Special Forces. I believe that's important to you. And if you're successful in the mission . . . I can't make promises, but I've been in preliminary conversations . . . there might be a presidential pardon for the way you shot up that town. So here's the question I have to ask you, Lieutenant: Are you in?"

"You're good," Rambo said. "You're really good."

"That doesn't answer my question."

"Yes. I'm in." Reflexively Rambo raised a hand to the scars beneath his denim shirt.

Murdock relaxed. "I'm glad that's settled. I'll get the necessary clearances."

"What's the plan?"

"Two phases. Recon and rescue. *You* are phase one. You will probe the site, confirm the presence of American POWs, if any, take photographic and tactical observations, then proceed to the extraction point." Murdock paused for emphasis. *"Without engaging the enemy."*

"Without . . . ?" Rambo stared from Murdock toward Trautman. "You're telling me I don't try to pull out any of our guys if I find them?"

Murdock didn't let Trautman answer. "Negative. Absolutely not. The phase-two assault team will get them out. Delta Force."

"But I'll be *there*. I can't believe . . . I just take pictures?"

"Don't look so disappointed, huh?" Murdock picked up his pen and tapped it on the desk. "This operation should be hairy enough." He narrowed his eyes. "Even for you."

"Sure. Photographs." Rambo turned to Trautman. "Sir, do we get to win this time?"

"This time," Trautman said, "it's up to you."

"Your flight to Bangkok," Murdock said, "is at oh-six-thirty. Commercial carrier. Low profile. Here's your passport, birth certificate, other supporting documents. You'll use your own name. That goes against my instincts, but the Thais these days are paying special attention to Americans when they come through customs. We don't want any . . . embarrassments, shall we say? But once you're in-country, we'll play a little more fast and loose with the rules." Murdock smiled as if that was the part he enjoyed.

Rambo studied his photograph in the passport. It was recent. It made him frown. He didn't recall when it had been taken. "Where'd you get this? You needed time to . . . You were that sure of me?"

"I'm sure of nothing. We could have shredded that stuff as easily as we had it made up," Murdock said. "In Bangkok, you'll rendezvous . . ."

— 2 —

The Japan Airlines jet's engines reduced their roar. The plane began its final approach, Rambo's stomach rising slightly, his eardrums swelling from the growing pressure behind them. He gritted his teeth and swallowed to clear them, hearing a pop, the sounds in the crowded cabin becoming more distinct. He saw clouds out his window, and then as the jet angled lower, he saw the picturesque Thailand countryside below him. Rain forest, farmland, rivers. And ahead, past the wing on this side, the sprawling flurry of Bangkok.

The last time he'd seen this part of the world had been when he glanced back through a window on a U.S. military carrier that was taking him back to the world, to the White House, to the Congressional Medal of Honor. His citation had described his escape from the Viet Cong prison camp and his six-week ordeal in the jungle as he struggled to reach American forces below the Demilitarized Zone. But no one, nothing, could ever truly describe what he'd been through. After having nearly been shot by American sentries who couldn't believe that anyone who looked as subhuman as he had could possibly be an American, he'd been flown by chopper for medical treatment in Saigon, and from there . . . Thirty-six hours later—talk about jet lag, culture shock, something—he'd landed at Edwards Air Force Base in the good old U.S. of A.

And then when he realized that everyone expected him to pick up the pieces of his life as if Nam had been an insignificant interruption, the true hell had started . . .

Leading him to that town.

And Teasle.

The jolt of the jet's wheels touching down brought Rambo back to the present. He picked up his travel bag—his only luggage—from beneath the forward seat.

And wondered why he didn't just stop right here. Just fade away.

After what he'd been through, he didn't owe anybody anything. The Orient was as familiar to him as the States. He could disappear. There'd be no more prisons. No more hassles.

Sure, why not?

But at once he thought of those POWs whose protracted hell made his own six months in captivity seem like a weekend.

And he thought of Trautman, who'd put his career on the line to get the "son" he'd trained released from walls that shrunk unbearably closer every night.

And breathing deeply, mustering resolve, he thought: All right, I gave my word. I'll honor it.

Just one more time.

But his stomach burned with apprehension as he passed the rigidly smiling stewardess—"Have a nice day. Thank you for flying with us"—and left the jet.

— 3 —

Bangkok's Don Muang Airport reminded him of a swarming ant's nest, but ants who used rancid cooking-oil, the smell of which was overwhelming. Walking inconspicuously among other departing passengers, he proceeded through mazelike corridors in the terminal to the customs area. His passport, as Murdock had said, was as clean as Kleenex.

"Purpose of your visit?"

"Pleasure."

The customs agent looked with disapproval, as if pleasure meant opium and whores.

But he stamped the passport. "Enjoy your stay."

And Rambo left the terminal.

Out front, he experienced the once familiar stifling heat of the Orient. Humidity clung to his forehead, drenching his shirt. His travel bag in hand, he stepped through throngs of Asians and tourists, scanning the chaos of traffic.

A beat-to-hell Citroën taxi hunkered low at the curb. Getting in, he told the lizard-faced driver to take him to the Indra Hotel.

But as soon as the taxi turned a corner, Rambo swung abruptly to check the traffic behind him. His muscles tensing, he quickly told the driver in Thai to stop.

The driver did, turning toward Rambo in the back, his eyebrows raised in puzzlement, making him look more lizardlike.

Rambo shoved ten dollars into his hand, grabbed the travel bag—*"Keep going. Now."*—and as the driver muttered, veering from the curb, Rambo lunged out, reminded vaguely of bailing out from an aircraft, assaulted by the din of the cluttered shopping district, at once absorbed by the crowd.

— 4 —

"You *what?* Let me try to understand this! You *lost* him, for Christ's sake?" Murdock clutched the microphone of a scrambler-protected two-way radio. The veins in his neck bulged. *"Three* of you? And you couldn't—?"

As static crackled, an apologetic voice blurted, "Hey, I'm sure he didn't notice us on the plane."

"I'll bet."

"I mean it. We looked like all the other tourists. Flowery shirts. Madras slacks. Straw hats. The whole enchilada."

"Christ," Murdock repeated.

"And none of us sat together. We followed him off the plane. Two of our local people were watching for him at customs. The surveillance car went after his taxi."

"And—?"

"The taxi suddenly stopped..."

"No, that's enough. I don't want to hear any more. The bunch of you fucked up is what it amounts to. Why and how don't matter."

"But I'm telling you, he never made one wrong move till—"

Murdock jerked his hand to shut off the voice. He scowled, raising his face, as if to God. "That asshole's going to love his next assignment. In Reykjavik, Iceland."

He seemed to remember he wasn't alone and swung toward Trautman. "And you . . . Correct me if I'm wrong. You guaranteed he'd show up. You said, 'I'll take the responsibility.' *Responsibility?* You want to talk about . . . ? Now that your full-bird colonel's rank is about to be clipped, how do you like . . . ?"

"He'll do what he promised." Trautman resisted the urge to suggest that Murdock perform an obscene act on himself.

Murdock blinked. "What he promised? He shoots up, *destroys,* an entire town, and you expect me to think he's just some Boy Scout who keeps his word?"

"That's the point. The town."

"Colonel, what we're having here is a problem of communication. I haven't the faintest idea what you're talking about."

"The town. Don't you see? That police chief did. What Rambo starts, he finishes."

"Finishes? He finished that town, all right. You sound like you're actually proud of what he did to it."

"Not proud." Trautman shook his head. "Proud isn't the word. Awestruck, maybe. You don't need to worry. I'm not sure why Rambo disappeared in Bangkok. But I'm sure he must have had a good reason. And I'm sure of this. He never went back on a promise, and he never broke a bargain. If he said he'd be here, he will be."

"Sir?" The voice belonged to a technician, who stared at a console in the background.

"Don't interrupt me," Murdock said.

"But, sir . . ."

"Well, dammit! What?"

"I've got a blip on the radar."

"What?"

"And, sir, it's headed this way."

— 5 —

The sunbathed golden Buddha loomed before him, its round unreadable face either blessing or damning. Hovering thirty feet off the ground, enjoying the tensely balanced stasis, Rambo studied the Buddha one more instant through the Plexiglas, then worked the controls, and with a sudden roaring surge, the chopper passed it.

After he'd left the taxi a block from the airport to disappear into the crowd, he'd darted down several streets at random. He'd hired another taxi and soon bailed out of it as well, shifting down teeming alleys to yet another taxi, proceeding in stages to the rendezvous at a farm on the edge of Bangkok. The old man who owned the farm would be his contact, Murdock had said, and after the old man removed the camouflage net, Rambo had found himself staring at a Vietnam-era Huey UH-1D, briefly associating it with—remembering—gunfire and screams.

Five minute later, Bangkok had been in the distance.

The Huey's shadow rippled over canals. Then a river. Temples, farmland, oxen. He pulled back the stick, and rice paddies disappeared as he rose to the clouds.

The once familiar controls were reassuring, though the memories they evoked were not, and he wondered if Murdock had chosen the Huey to put him back in a wartime frame of mind. If so, the tactic had worked.

And he resented the manipulation.

But at the moment, resentment and even memories of

the war didn't matter. His sense of freedom, being up here, floating, drifting, made his chest swell. As if in charge of his own private roller coaster, he swooped down through the clouds, feeling his stomach rise. At once his stomach settled as he leveled off above the rain forest.

He smiled and cleared a mountaintop. Recalling the first car he'd ever owned, a battered blue '63 Ford—and the drag strip back in Bowie, Arizona—he made the chopper do what the Ford could never have done and descended through the morning haze.

Only to sober as he saw his destination.

Below, a military base was spread out. An airstrip cut through a meadow flanked by forested slopes. Beyond, wreathed in clouds, mountains followed mountains, disappearing into the distance with increasingly paler shades of gray like an Oriental watercolor.

The base seemed abandoned, its hangars and smaller buildings rusty, vine-covered, a neglected vestige of the war. But as he came nearer, lower, he saw that the airstrip was in perfect shape, and that men were crowded at the entrance to one hangar. Two stepped out, one in uniform, the other in rolled-up shirt sleeves, a tie hanging loose, the civilian walking faster, leaving his companion far behind as he stalked impatiently in this direction.

The landing pad was near the hangar. Taking pride in the gentle touch that he hadn't forgotten, Rambo eased the Huey down. Dust flew, settling as he shut off the power. The rotors whined to a stop. He slipped off his headset and climbed down from the pilot's seat. After the flapping roar of the chopper, the base seemed terribly quiet.

"What the"—Murdock, his armpits drenched with sweat, charged up to him, Trautman following—"fuck do you think you're—?

"Reporting as requested, sir."

"Requested?" Murdock's voice rose. *"Requested?* Don't pretend you didn't . . . What about that stunt in Bangkok?"

Rambo looked puzzled. "Stunt?"

"Losing your—" Murdock suddenly stopped.

"What's the matter, Murdock?" Trautman asked, arriving. "Don't you want to admit that you had him followed?"

"Followed?" Rambo reacted with apparent surprise. "But I don't get it. Why would you have me followed? I reported at the rendezvous. That farm."

Murdock groaned.

"Sure, John, you reported to the rendezvous. But just supposing," Trautman said.

Murdock glanced from Rambo to Trautman, puzzled.

"For the sake of discussion," Trautman said, "supposing you knew you were being followed; and supposing you ditched them before you got to the rendezvous . . . Why?"

"We're just being hypothetical?" Rambo asked.

"That's right. Hypothetical."

"Well, I suppose if I knew I was being followed, anybody else could have spotted them, too. You said it yourself— the Thais are paying close attention to Americans these days. If I ditched a friendly tail, I'd also be losing an *un*friendly tail. And, after all, you wouldn't want anybody to know where I was going."

Murdock squinted. "Cute. That's very cute."

"But as the colonel says, we're just being hypothetical. I wouldn't want to make your people nervous."

"But since we're supposing," Trautman said, "can you think of any other reason you might want to lose a tail?"

"Sir?"

"For example, to prove that you didn't *have* to be followed? That you weren't forced? That you came on your own?"

"I wouldn't know anything about that, sir."

And Murdock repeated, "Oh, that's cute."

They stared at each other.

"Well . . ." Trautman cleared his throat. "Unless you want to keep arguing, Murdock, I suggest we get back under cover. After all, this base *is* supposed to look abandoned."

Murdock nodded, apparently glad to change the subject,

reasserting his authority. "And now that Audie Murphy here has finally arrived, we'd better get this damned Huey out of sight." He walked briskly ahead of them toward the wide dark opening of the hangar.

"John . . ." Trautman shook his head.

"Sir"—Rambo smiled—"the devil made me do it."

As he followed Murdock, he glanced around. On the right, a camouflage canopy hid a large all-black Agusta 109 helicopter. It squatted ominously, no markings, its contents shielded. Two mechanics checked its back rotor. Otherwise, the base looked innocent.

He frowned and entered the shadowy hangar, and even before his eyes adjusted, he stopped, impressed.

The huge metal building actually hummed. The walls subtly vibrated. A mass of electronic equipment was clustered before him.

Ghostly in the dark, banks of video monitors glowed. Green letters gave off an eerie light on computer screens. Radar bands gleamed as they swept around on their grids. Work stations for tracking, communications, and long-range coordination formed a complex jumble on modular equipment racks, almost like a room within the hangar.

And in the background, he heard . . .

"Who . . . what's . . . that?" a technician asked.

"The one going in," another technician said.

"Going in? Christ, he looks like he just came out."

Beyond the technicians, past a row of glowing equipment, Rambo saw Murdock talking urgently to a man . . . who nodded and came his way.

A tall sharp-featured American, wearing jeans, an air force shirt with the sleeves torn off at the shoulders, tattoos on his biceps, and a Dodgers baseball cap.

He tipped it, grinning. "Hi, my name's Ericson, and welcome to hell."

Rambo studied him as if he'd encountered a strange new species.

But Ericson didn't seem to notice. He just kept grinning.

"So you're the chosen one, huh? Lucky guy. I'll tell you, this is the worst assignment I've had so far. One of these days, maybe they'll send me to the south of France, huh?"

"Yeah, right. South of France."

"It's 'Rambo,' correct? Man, I've heard a lot about you. Made some hot moves. I like that. Lets me know where you're coming from."

"Yeah? Where's that?"

"Never mind. I'll catch you later. Right now, I've got to move that Huey out of sight." Ericson rushed forward past Rambo toward the chopper outside. "By the way, I'm your escort service."

"What?"

Outside the hangar, Ericson turned, running backward like a football player. "Your pilot! Hey, think of the setup this way! This place may not be heaven, but at least you got sprung from prison!"

"Did I?" Frowning, Rambo watched Ericson scramble into the Huey. Frowning harder, he turned to Trautman. ". . . Pilot?"

But Murdock was suddenly there. He opened his mouth. Rambo spoke first. "How long have you been setting up?"

Murdock looked suspicious, as if the question was somehow a threat, as if anything he answered would be treated with ridicule. "How long? Well, let me . . . See, we had some foul-ups coming in." Peeling his sweaty shirt from his ample chest, he answered defensively, "Twenty-two hours. On site."

Rambo glanced around, nodding. "Nice work."

And Murdock's chest inflated. He gestured proudly toward a cubicle in back. "Step into my orifice."

— 6 —

The room was ten feet wide, enclosed by crudely assembled plywood. It had a metal desk upon which a tensor lamp glowed past a computer screen and keyboard toward stacks of official-looking documents. There were three metal chairs, a row of metal filing cabinets, a glaring overhead light, a humidity-wrinkled map on the wall, two humming fans, and a Coca-Cola machine.

Their footsteps echoed as they came in. The room smelled musty. Murdock gestured toward the map on the wall, began to explain, had second thoughts about something, and turned.

"Before I start this briefing, I think there's something we'd better get settled, Rambo. You and I got off on the wrong foot, so to speak. I admit it. At the prison. At Bragg." He nodded toward the door. "Out there. So you don't like what you call 'spooks.' That's fine. You've no doubt got your reasons. But don't be quick to judge. Because you certainly don't know as much about me as I do about you. For what it's worth, I was honching with the Second Battalion, Third Marines, at Qon Thien in '66. And I wasn't one of those chicken-shit officers who hangs back while his men lead the way. I saw combat. Plenty. I've got several Purple Hearts. And at night I can still hear the screams of the men who served with me and got killed. So believe me, I know what you and every other vet feel. At the time, maybe the government didn't seem to care. Maybe certain sectors of the public didn't care. But things are different now. The *country's* different. People care, and Congress cares, and you can bet the committee who sent me over here cares. In retrospect, it may have been a bad war. But those men, those *soldiers,* weren't bad. And that's what matters. So"—Murdock spoke faster, compelled by emotion—"I suggest we put away our personal differences and do our damnedest to get those POWs out of there. *Back home where they belong.*"

His voice shook.

Moved, Rambo nodded.

"Good. I think we'll both feel a lot better now," Murdock said. "I'm glad that's out of the way. But something else. I want to emphasize that with your unique qualifications, your special skills, I feel this mission has a better-than-average . . . no, that's wrong . . . a *superior* chance of succeeding where others have failed. I'm delighted to have you aboard."

Murdock held out his hand and grinned. "The last time I did this, you were, well, uh, somewhat inconvenienced."

Rambo had to grin as well. He studied the outstretched hand.

And shook with him.

"Now let's get down to business." Again Murdock turned to the map, which detailed this section of Southeast Asia. He jabbed a finger at each area, moving on a slightly upward angle, from left to right. "Thailand. The Mekong River. Laos. Nam. You'll be flown northeast, a straight dash through the Laotian panhandle. Then through the Annamese Mountains and on up to the drop zone. Eighteen minutes in Communist airspace." Murdock raised his eyebrows. "Does that give you any problems?"

"Eighteen minutes? No. But going in, I assume the plane'll fly low to stay off their radar."

"Low isn't quite the word. You'll be down so close you could mow the lawn."

"In the rhubarb. Yeah, I expected."

"But even at the drop zone," Murdock said. "I want to be clear about this. At the insertion site, the most we can give you is a ceiling of two hundred and fifty feet when you leave the plane. Can you handle that?"

Rambo shrugged. "Depends."

"On what?"

"Well, do I get to use a parachute?"

Murdock's face went blank. He glanced puzzled at Trautman, who started laughing.

"Do you get to use a—?" Murdock asked. "Well, I'll be damned."

A technician appeared at the open door.

"What is it?" Murdock asked. "Can't you see I'm—?"

"Sure, but we've got a problem."

"We've all got problems. You'll just have to deal with it."

"Not without your help. You have to—"

"Can't it wait?"

"No, not if you want to keep on schedule. The computer's giving us garbage. You've got so many anti-intruder locks in the programs, I need you to double-check the access codes."

"It's okay. Go with him," Trautman said. "I'll finish the briefing."

Murdock nodded gratefully and left the office.

For a moment, the only sound was the humming of the two rotating fans.

"How are you feeling?" Trautman asked.

Rambo held out his hand, palm flat. It was steady.

"I might have known."

"So what's the rest of the deal?"

"The code name for the insertion and extraction flight team is 'Dragonfly.' Home base—here—is 'Wolf Den.' Your code name is 'Lone Wolf.' Since you're going solo, you'll have to rely on more equipment than you've ever used before. And I do mean rely. Forget the blood-and-guts routine. Take it easy for a change. Let technology do most of the work. If you need assistance, all you have to do is call for it."

"Like 'let your fingers do the walking.'"

"Affirmative." Trautman smiled. "Come on. I want to show you something."

— 7 —

They left the office, heading past technicians and gleaming equipment toward the rear of the shadowy hangar.

"So what do you think?" Trautman asked with a sweeping gesture. "There's your ride."

Rambo found himself staring at a sleek—distressingly so—all-black jet, a modified Gulfstream Peregrine, the single-engine executive model. All insignia and I.D. numbers had been removed. It looked like a rocket with wings.

"Impressed?" Murdock asked, coming over.

Turning, Rambo watched him approach.

"And the Peregrine isn't all," Murdock said. "Besides the monitoring devices you saw when you came in, you'll be issued every ultra-modern piece of equipment available—to ensure your safety. I know that a lot of this is new to you, Rambo. Warfare has come a long way since you were in the book. But that's to the good. You can feel totally secure because today we have weapons so advanced that what you used in Nam will seem like spears and slingshots."

"Sure," Rambo said. He didn't like being made to feel antiquated. "That's the thing about weapons. They always get more advanced. But what if—? See, sometimes equipment gets lost or doesn't work. And then what? At Bragg, I was taught"—Rambo pointed at Trautman—"by *him* . . . that the best weapon's always the mind."

"Times change," Murdock said.

"For *some* people."

"This is true. But don't let me interrupt, Colonel." Murdock folded his arms.

"After insertion," Trautman said, "you'll contact base camp. With this."

He walked to an olive-drab box that sat on a crate. The box resembled the type of compact field radio that Rambo had used in the war, with the difference that an unfamiliar complex console was set in the top.

"This is called a transponder-satellite relay," Trautman said. "TRANSAT for short. To make it work, you have to use this."

He opened a small collapsible dish antenna, attached it to a tripod, and plugged a cord from the tripod into the TRANSAT box.

"The message you send will go out in what's called a burst. All in less than a second. In fact, a milisecond. The signal's coded into an infrared pulse, picked up by our spy satellite, bounced to the ground station in Okinawa, and relayed back to here. We slow it down and decode it."

"Makes sense," Rambo said. "No radio source. Nothing for the enemy to triangulate on."

"And as soon as you've sent the message letting us know that you're down and safe, you'll proceed through the forest to point Tango November." He held up a field map. "It's clearly marked. There you'll rendezvous with your ground contact. Indigenous agent. Co Phuong Bao."

Rambo glanced, distressed by something that unconsciously nagged at him, that he couldn't quite specify, that as Murdock might have said didn't quite compute, toward the Peregrine jet.

"Is he listening?" Murdock asked.

"Indigenous agent," Rambo said. "Co Phuong Bao. Keep going."

"The guide will take you twelve klicks upriver to your target at Ban Kia Na."

"The camp." Remembering, Rambo felt his stomach shrink.

"Where you'll take photographs," Murdock interrupted again. "I repeat. Photographs. Your phase of the operation does not involve rescue, only reconnaissance. If those POWs are there, we'll get them out. It's not your job. With the photographs, you'll proceed downriver to the extraction site at point Echo Delta marked on your map. Ericson will bring you back with that Agusta chopper you saw under wraps beside the hangar."

"And we all live happily ever after," Rambo said.

"Yeah, right, happily ever after. But do you *understand?* Is everything clear?"

"Why not?"

"And now for your weapons," Murdock said proudly. He reached inside a crate and held up an enormous raygun-like assault rifle with huge cylinders below and above the barrel, which along with an exotic telescopic sight made it look like—

"Something out of *Star Wars,*" Rambo said. "I can't take that thing. It's as big as a Chrysler."

"Because it takes the place of a half dozen other weapons. This is a modified M-16 A2 and over-under M-79 grenade launcher. It's got a Sionics sound suppressor, a Tracor star-light scope, and an LAC/R-100 laser sighting system. It's also got a mount for your high-resolution camera."

"But are the batteries included? Look, Murdock, that's very impressive. I'm sure it works well in the lab. But what I could really use is an AK-47."

"Hell, every twelve-year-old in Nam's got one of those."

"And that's the point. In a firefight, they won't hear any difference between the sound of my weapon and their own. So they won't know who they're shooting at, me or them. Maybe they'll even shoot at each other. And I won't have trouble finding ammunition."

Murdock glanced at the huge contorted assault rifle like a kid disappointed that Rambo didn't like his toy. "Well, all right, then. If you insist on being . . . In that case, I've got just the thing for you. I mean, it's right up your alley. You're going to cream. You remember I told you that a weapon like this makes the stuff you used in Nam seem like spears and slingshots? Then here, you'd better take this."

From the crate, Murdock pulled out a two-foot-long, six-inch-wide aluminum tube. He tossed it over.

Catching it, Rambo hefted it—the tube didn't weigh much—and frowned. "So what is it?"

"A goddamned bow and arrow."

"Well, now you're talking."

— 8 —

As Rambo left the shadows of the hangar, his muscular body silhouetted by sunlight, opening the end of the tube, preparing to practice, Murdock turned to Trautman and shook his head with doubt.

"Colonel, are you sure he's not still unhinged from the war? That joke he made about the parachute. And he's actually—I can't believe this. I mean I really have my doubts—more interested in a bow and arrow than in a state-of-the-art grenade launcher. We can't afford to have anyone involved who might crack under pressure in hostile territory."

"Pressure?" Trautman looked stunned. "I thought you said you studied his file, that you know all about him. He's the best combat soldier I've ever seen. Even at Bragg during his training, it was obvious he was a natural. A genius. He's got an instinct for fighting, and right now only one desire—to win a war someone else forced him to lose."

"Colonel, come on now, you disappoint me. I hope you're not going back to that old chestnut about the government holding the military's arms so it couldn't win."

"Lies were told. And good men died because of it. And other good men are still being held captive because of it. And Rambo—well, if winning now means he has to die as well, he'll die. No fear. No regrets. That more than anything is what makes him special. Crack under pressure? No way. Because, Murdock, what you choose to call hostile territory..."

"Yeah? What about it?"

"He calls it home."

– 3 –

THE WAT

— I —

Outside, a rising whine turned into a steady roar. It made the plywood walls of this narrow room—they reminded him of his prison cell—begin to tremble. Peregrine was out there, getting ready for flight.

Before him, his equipment was spread out on a metal table, illuminated by a tensor light.

Naked, his scrotum tensed against his abdomen, he studied everything.

He put on tiger-stripe cammies, tied his jump boots, and streaked his face and hands with two shades of green camouflage makeup.

He removed his survival knife from its scabbard, honing it once more on the pencil-sized diamond sharpener that fit in a loop on the sheath. The knife was to him as beautiful a weapon as the combination M-16/grenade launcher had been to Murdock. The blade was ten inches long, made from 440C stainless steel, virtually unbreakable, its cutting edge razor-sharp. It had the shape of a Bowie knife. Two inches wide, one quarter of an inch thick, it weighed one and three-quarter pounds. The reverse side of the cutting edge had deep, wide, sawlike serrations capable of cutting through the fuselage of an aircraft or the corrugated walls of this hangar. Its handle was stainless steel, wrapped with one hundred and twenty pound testweight fishing line. The handle was five inches long, increasing the overall length of the knife to fifteen inches. For a medium-sized adult, it would stretch from the elbow to the tips of the fingers. The guard on the handle had a one-inch extension on each side of the blade. One extension had a Phillips screwdriver head. The other had a conventional straight screwdriver head. Behind the head of each screwdriver, a hole through the metal allowed him to lash the knife securely to a pole, using leather thongs from the sheath, to make the knife a spear. The end could be unscrewed from the hollow handle, the inside part of the cap a liquid-filled magnetic compass. The compartment within the handle contained a tiny razor-sharp folding knife, matches in a waterproof container, fishhooks, and a needle which he could use along with the fishing line to suture himself. Indeed, he had sutured himself many times. The most recent occasion had been when Teasle's posse had wounded him during his escape through the mountains outside that town. The scar on his left biceps constantly reminded him. Grim, he bit his lip.

After he finished honing the knife, he normally would have lit a match and drawn the flame along the shiny blade, expertly letting the carbon from the smoke darken the metal, lest the blade's reflecting glint be a liability at night during combat. But in this case, he didn't need to do so. Because the blade was already black, electrochemically treated to retain a dark matte finish.

He loaded and inspected the AK-47, once more checking its sights. He inserted .45 hollow-point rounds into a magazine and shoved the magazine into the handle of a Colt pistol, pulling back the slide, chambering a round, easing the hammer down, and securing the safety catch. He shoved the pistol into a holster at his side and loaded two other magazines, taping them to each arm.

"D minus ten minutes," an echoing metallic voice said over a loudspeaker out there in the hangar.

He turned to the sound, thought a moment, then stepped to a corner of this compartment, sat and crossed his legs, assuming a Buddha position. He stared at a portion of the shadowy roof above across from him and focused on a spider web. Imagining that he was a spider on that web, he focused on a strand of silk within the web, and then imagining that he was a microorganism upon that strand of silk, he cleared his mind so he could meditate about infinity. Receding within himself, he became a black hole.

A sound brought him back.

He blinked, his soul expanding. Tap, tap. Knuckles rapping on his door.

He frowned as the door creaked open. Red and blue lights flashed out there. A silhouette appeared.

He resisted the interruption. Where he'd been—within the organism upon the strand of silk upon the spider web across from him on the ceiling—had been incredibly peaceful.

But then he realized who stood in the doorway. Trautman. And he nodded.

Indeed, with affection he almost smiled.

"Time, John."

"Sure."

Rambo stood. He put on his parachute, which of course he'd packed himself. He slung the AK-47 over one shoulder. He approached two leather quivers on the table. Both were twenty-two inches long, sealed with a strap-down leather cap. One contained his bow, the other his arrows. He buckled these to each thigh, making him look like a gunslinger.

"Let me help with the rest," Trautman said and slung the TRANSAT drab-olive box across his chest. He studied Rambo drolly. "Murdock's got you so loaded down you'd think you were set for a weekend in Vegas. We'd better not forget the camera."

"How I spent my summer vacation."

"If you get any girlie shots, I've got dibs on seeing them first."

"It's a deal."

Their smiles subdued, they left the compartment.

The blue and red flashing lights become more vivid, intensifying as he walked from the hangar, approaching Peregrine.

Murdock, technicians, and military personnel stood to the right.

Trautman stopped and turned to face him. "John..." Whatever he meant to say, he seemed to change his mind, becoming less emotional, more professional. "Thirty-six hours to get the hell in and out, so don't stop to smell the roses, okay?"

Rambo nodded.

"Any trouble, I mean *any* trouble, let us know and get your ass to the alternate Hawk September extraction point that's marked on your map. Okay?"

Again he nodded.

Peregrine's lights flashed insistently. Unseen behind them, Ericson yelled, barely audible in the roar from the engine, "Colonel, we're ready to roll!"

Trautman waved to the jet and turned. "Good luck... son."

Rambo's voice was low and hard. "Remember when Murdock said he was with the Second Battalion, Third Marines, at Con Thien in '66?"

"What about it?"

"The Second Battalion was at *Kud Sank*."

"Well," Trautman said, "he must have misremembered."

"Some things you don't—you can't—you *never*—forget."

"What you mean is *you* don't."

"You don't either."

Trautman tapped him on the shoulder.

It was enough. As much as their way of life allowed for the demonstration of affection.

Rambo nodded.

And stalked toward Peregrine.

— 2 —

His throat constricting, Trautman watched him climb inside the jet.

The hatch went shut. At once the engine roared louder, blasting flame, taxiing toward the takeoff position on the runway. With unexpected suddenness, the jet lunged forward, deafening, hurtling down the runway, gathering speed. Its nose picked up. It cleared the end and then the tree line, or in the dark what seemed to be the tree line.

And abruptly vanished.

The night was strangely still.

His stomach feeling hollow, he turned toward the hangar.

And Murdock was standing behind him.

"You think he'll find anybody?" After the roar of the jet, Trautman's voice sounded unnatural.

"POWs? Doubtful." Murdock shrugged. "But there are people to satisfy. And questions that have to be answered."

"You don't sound too emotional about it," Trautman said.

"It wasn't my war, Colonel. I'm just here to clean up the mess."

— 3 —

Peregrine's roaring jet made a humming sound through the fuselage. Except for a single red light above the bail-out door, the passenger compartment was dark. Sitting once more in a Buddha position, Rambo stared at the glowing front of the aircraft.

Up there, next to Ericson, who handled the controls, another man, Doyle—after introductions, Rambo had decided that Doyle's deranged eyes were the consequence of too many methane weekends—checked the HUD display that reflected instrument readings onto the cockpit windshield, allowing the crew to check the readouts without ever looking down at the panel.

Peregrine's roaring jet continued to hum through the fuselage.

Rambo ignored it, once more on that spider's web.

— 4 —

Tensely hunched beside a console in the hangar, Trautman stared at a radar screen, oblivious to Murdock, next to him.

"AWACS two-five has acquired," an earphoned technician announced. "They are holding time line." The technician spoke into his microphone. "Affirmative, Lone Wolf. Over."

Trautman stared harder at the radar . . .

At the glowing dot that represented Peregrine as the jet seemed to crawl almost imperceptibly across a computer-generated grid of central Laos.

The glowing dot, like a laser, burned his eyes.

— 5 —

Sensing movement in the cockpit, Rambo lifted his consciousness from the imaginary spider web. As a blurred image suddenly focuses, he found himself in Peregrine's interior.

Ahead, silhouetted by the glow of instruments, Ericson was standing. He let Doyle handle the controls and squeezed past his seat to come this way, his outline blending with the dark. "You don't want to miss this. Have a look."

Rambo stood and followed him, stopping between the pilot and copilot seat. To the right, Doyle was hunched forward, his nose inches from the canopy. To the left, Ericson buckled in and took over the controls.

Through the windshield, Rambo saw only darkness for a moment. Then his eyes adjusted, and moonlight made the rain forest spread out below him glow eerily. Thickly leaved trees, dense, crowded, seemed to rush beneath him at astonishing speed.

"Now comes the sexy part," Ericson said. He switched off the instrument lights.

The cockpit went totally dark.

And ahead, jagged, towering, filling the horizon from one end to the other, a chiaroscuro emphasized by the moon, was the massive Annamese mountain range.

One moment the range seemed in the distance. The next it loomed directly in front, and Ericson pushed the controls, streaking down. He followed the rippling contour of the foothills. He snaked through a twisting canyon, mountains suddenly on each side. He made the Peregrine slither between their flanks.

Beside him, Doyle giggled and switched on a penlight, aiming its tiny beam toward the instruments so Ericson could read them.

But Ericson was far beyond the need to read instruments. He and Peregrine were one. The roar from the airstream outside sounded awesome.

Ericson let out a rebel yell. "Whoo-ya! I love it!" Despite his seat belt, he squirmed excitedly.

Doyle giggled again. "Punch it! Gimme more gees!"

Rambo felt his stomach pushing toward his back.

And as quickly as the mountains had loomed, they disappeared, replaced by another rush of dense, eerie rain forest. Though it seemed impossible to do, Ericson hugged the Peregrine even closer to the treetops.

"Back in the badlands, my man," he said.

The rain forest looked no different from its counterparts in Thailand and Laos. But—Rambo's muscles hardened—this was Nam. In-country. And that made *all* the difference.

"Party time," Doyle said.

Ericson nodded. "She's yours." He unbuckled and stood, adjusting his earphone set. "Better saddle up," he told Rambo. "Insertion in minus one minute."

Rambo's heart sped. At once he concentrated and brought it back to normal. Forty-two beats per minute. He turned and walked back to the passenger compartment.

Ericson opened the door. The buffeting roar was deafening.

Rambo squinted. After one last equipment check, he

hooked his static line to the rod above his head.

Outside, the rain forest swept by, so close that leaves were distinguishable in the moonlight.

The red light above him changed to yellow. Rambo took a breath.

"Five seconds," Ericson said. "Four. Three. Two. One. Have a nice night."

The yellow light turned to green.

"Go," Ericson said.

And with a single powerful stride, Rambo leaped through the open door.

Gone.

— 6 —

"Jesus Christ!" Trautman heard from the radio. The voice belonged to Ericson, panicked.

Murdock straightened. "What the hell? What's happening?"

A pulsing alarm blared from the speaker.

"Oh, shit! Oh, Jesus fucking Christ!" Ericson blurted from the radio.

"What's *happening?*" Murdock repeated. He grabbed the microphone. "Dragonfly! Come in, Dragonfly!"

"His static line! Oh, Jesus, fuck, he's hung up!" Ericson shouted from the radio.

"He's *what?*"

"Condition red! His line didn't separate from the chute! He's being dragged!"

Trautman dug his fingernails into his palms.

"Release the line!" Murdock yelled.

"I can't! It won't . . . !"

"For Christ's sake, cut it!"

"Can't! I don't have a knife! Oh, motherfuck, he's being torn apart out there!"

Trautman's hands felt sticky. Peering down, he saw that his fingernails drew blood from his palms.

"Condition red! Condition . . . !"

— 7 —

As he leaped through the open doorway, feeling sudden weightlessness, his stomach expanding, Rambo had winced from the unexpected brutal jerk. His shoulders were yanked so hard that he feared they'd be dislocated from their sockets. The pain was overwhelming. He walloped against the side of the fuselage, gasped and dropped, his equipment tangling. As he was dragged along, twisting, turning, an arm's length from Peregrine's belly, so close to the treetops that they threatened to rake his guts out, he realized with alarm what had happened. His static line. It hadn't pulled free. It hadn't jerked loose to open his chute.

The wind velocity was agonizing. It tore off his helmet. It forced air down his throat. He couldn't expel it, couldn't breathe.

The G-force pinned his arms to his sides. The weight of all his equipment threatened to crush him.

Pull the chute cord, he thought frantically. But then he realized that if he got the chute open—and if the static line remained attached to it—he'd become caught even worse on the jet, this time by the chute itself.

Peregrine's roaring engine—combined with the din of the jetstream—threatened to burst his eardrums. His AK-47 was torn from its position on his shoulder, dragged down his helpless arm, cascading free toward the unseen rain forest. Something gave way on his TRANSAT radio's cinching. It, too, was yanked away, spinning below him, disappearing toward the shadowy trees.

Breathe. Oh, my God, I've got to breathe.

— 8 —

Doyle winced from the roar in the cockpit, the raucous blare of the pulsing alarm, and stared ahead through the canopy, his mouth hanging open, gasping at another set of mountains streaking toward him.

He shouted to his microphone, to Ericson. "I've gotta climb! We've gotta pull out!"

"Not yet!"

"But these goddamned mountains . . . !"

"He's trying something! For Christ's sake, not yet!"

— 9 —

Rambo's muscles resisted. Straining his arm, he managed to get it in motion. The darkness in which he was being dragged was bad enough, but the force of the wind added to his blindness. He had to do this by feel. Inch by inch, in agony from the effort, his arm cramping fiercely, he groped toward the knife on his belt.

Breathe. If only he could...

Months of raising the heavy sledgehammer, of thrusting it down with all his strength, of shattering those incredibly vivid beautiful rocks, had developed his muscles into rock-like contours of their own. Mustering their full power, he gripped the vise of his fingers around the handle of his knife, unsnapped its strap, and slowly tugged it free.

His chest ached, lungs burning, demanding air.

But freeing the knife had been the easy part. A survivor of Nam, of the prison camp, that town and yet another prison, he felt now as if challenged by the truly impossible.

To raise his hand beyond his head.

And then he got mad.

— 10 —

Trautman stopped breathing. Oblivious to the hangar, the instruments, and Murdock beside him, he concentrated only on the radio, the speakers, the urgent voices, transporting his imagination into Peregrine itself, standing at the open doorway, watching paralyzed as Rambo was dragged through the night.

"He's got his knife!" Ericson blurted.

"We have to pull out!" Doyle shouted.

"No! He's doing it! Jesus Christ, he's doing it! He's cutting the static cord!"

"I can't wait any longer! These goddamned mountains!"

"He's gone!"

"What?"

"Out!"

"Out where? Did he get his chute to pop open?"

"Hey, man, who the hell knows?"

Trautman flicked his tongue along his dry lips. He waited, tense. Come on. Pull that rip cord. *Pull it*.

The radio became silent.

Two hundred and fifty feet to the forest, Trautman thought frantically. Seconds to the ground. If he made it, he'll call in. Half a minute, max.

But thirty seconds lengthened to a minute.

Come on, he thought.

Murdock frowned at an earphoned technician.

The technician shook his head. "Nothing's coming in from him, sir. All I get is static."

Come on!

"The frequency seems to be dead."

Trautman grabbed the microphone from him. "Dragonfly, this is Wolf Den. Do you read me? Over."

Ericson's voice burst through the static. "Come in, Wolf Den. This is Dragonfly. Over."

"Any signal from him? Visual bearings by flares?"

"Negative, sir," Ericson said. "And we're way past the drop zone. I didn't see a thing. Do you want us to make a second pass?"

Next to Trautman, Murdock fiercely shook his head. "We can't afford the exposure. If the Communists shoot down that jet, then we've *really* got our ass in a sling."

Trautman frowned, considering. The professional in him took over. "Negative, Dragonfly. Repeat—negative. Do not make a second pass. Return to Wolf Den."

"Roger, Wolf Den. Over. Out."

Trautman set down the microphone. Despite the hum of the instruments in the hangar, the massive area felt deathly quiet. Technicians and military personnel gathered around, terribly silent.

Murdock cupped a hand to his mouth, debating, his forehead deeply furrowed. He lowered his hand. "I don't know," he said. "Maybe the smart thing to do is abort the mission now—before we have any more complications. Pack up. Get the hell out."

"No," Trautman said.

"But I mean, who could've survived something like that?"

"If anybody could . . ."

"He could? Colonel, I appreciate your loyalty. I respect it. But for all your faith in him, he's still just a man. We have to be practical."

Trautman raised his voice. "He's got to be given the benefit of the doubt. Anything could have happened. His radio might have been damaged. We made a bargain with him, and by Christ, we're keeping it. Thirty-six hours to carry out the mission and reach the extraction site. If he's alive but he can't communicate with us, he'll still do the job. And he'll count on us doing ours. *We owe him that.*"

Murdock stared. His jawline slowly softened. "Of course we do." He squinted. "But understand. Thirty-six hours. That's the end of our bargain . . . and then we pull out."

"Of course. He'd expect no more. And no less."

— || —

As Rambo's chute exploded open, Peregrine was suddenly gone, the flame from its afterburner vanishing like the off-blink of a firefly in the night. As well, the roar was gone, the din of the wind. He felt the yank of the parachute on his harness, and as his speed reduced, his stomach regaining its equilibrium, he floated.

The soothing sensation was deceptive. With wind-caused tears blurring his eyes, he couldn't see the rain forest below him, but touchdown would be alarmingly soon. The trick now was to press his legs as tightly together as his muscular thighs would allow. The maximum risk of jumping into thickly wooded terrain, especially at night, was that your legs would separate and you'd land hard, straddling a tree limb . . . and split your body straight up the middle, one half toppling this way, the other . . . blood gushing . . .

Rambo shut the image from his mind, continuing to squeeze his legs shut. A heavy branch whisked past him. His shoulder scraped a bough. His chute snagged, jerked him—but at least it slowed his descent—then tore free, dropping him for a sudden five feet, then another. Bracing himself for the landing he couldn't anticipate, he gasped from the shock of his boots touching down.

His knees were already bent, absorbing the impact. Automatically he curved his body, rolling sideways. Onto what? His shoulder whacked over a log. Still rolling, he rustled through ferns, bumped across another log, and walloped to an agonizing stop against a tree.

The impact so stunned him that he had to lie there for a moment, letting his senses adjust, his muscles relax. A tremor shook him.

And then, despite the pain in his back, he felt ready. Crouching smoothly, he hauled in his chute, glancing on guard around him, straining to penetrate the gloom of the rain forest. Animals skittered through branches. Monkeys screeched. Then the night was still.

Compacting his chute, he stuffed it beneath a log, concealing it with ferns. The stifling humidity enveloped him, making his camouflage clothes cling slick to his sweaty chest and arms and legs. He felt as if he breathed through a steaming washrag.

Equipment check.

He'd lost his rifle, his camera, his TRANSAT radio.

No way to communicate with base. No way to . . . How would they know he'd survived? How would they know that they still had to pick him up in thirty-six hours?

No. He had to stop thinking like that. If Murdock was the only man running the show, he knew he'd have a right to worry.

But Trautman . . . Trautman was back there, too. And Trautman he could count on. The pickup team would be there as promised.

And he himself would do the mission as promised.

His momentary doubt was gone.

All right, he knew what he'd lost. But what did he *have?* His knife. His pistol.

The two quivers strapped to his thighs. Despite the circumstances, Rambo had to grin, remembering Murdock's astonishment when he'd rejected the over-under M-16 grenade launcher. In favor of . . . ?

Here, Murdock had said. You want the equivalent of spears and slingshots? This'll be right up your alley.

A bow and arrow.

Rambo stood. His eyes had now adjusted to the night. Moonlight filtered down through the drooping foliage of the massive trees. Its scattered beams were eerie glowing shafts in the swirling night mist.

This rain forest was among the most primeval in the world, a welter of violent growth and death-filled shadows. Massive tree roots gripped the earth as if strangling it. Twisting vines climbed swaying into the vaulted canopy above. Water dripped constantly.

And he sensed life everywhere. Furtive. Prehistoric. Churning in the shallow pools, under logs, indeed within their bark, in the sweating fruit, leaping through the matted leaves above.

He drew his knife, untwisted the cap on its handle, and cupped his hand over the subtle glow of the phosphorescent compass. He didn't dare strike a match to read the waterproof map in his back pocket. But he'd memorized the coordinates toward which he'd have to move, and for the moment, as he studied the luminous needle on his compass, he decided that he couldn't go wrong if he started in the general direction of his rendezvous sight.

Northeast.

Deeper into Nam.

He nodded, determined, wraithlike, shifting through the undergrowth.

— 12 —

At dawn, the mazelike obstacles of the rain forest becoming more distinct, he struggled up a steep hill, grabbing vines and tree roots for leverage, lunging onto level ground at the top. Catching his breath, he once more checked his compass. From this ridgeline, the sun gleaming higher, he was able to see the features of the deceptively beautiful overgrown valley below him. Comparing what he saw to the topographical features on his map, he now located his position, slightly altered his direction, and moved precisely toward the rendezvous site, descending the ridge.

Through claustrophobic undergrowth, he reached a sluggish stream, stepping off the muddy bank, wading through the tepid, knee-deep scummy water. Clouds of mosquitoes attacked his face, tickling his eyelids, buzzing up his nostrils, irritating. But by now he was used to them. And he'd shoved malaria-fighting suppositories up his anus. Knowing it would do no good to swat at the insects, he didn't.

On the opposite bank, he paused to roll up his pant legs. Fat, liverlike bloodsuckers clung to his shins. He removed a small plastic pouch of salt from his shirt pocket, swallowing some of it, not tasting its bitterness—which meant that he needed it—then dabbing salt on each bloodsucker, the white grotesque against their pulsing black. It gave him satisfaction to see them squirm.

One fell away. The others writhed and soon dropped as well. He crushed them with his boot, feeling them squish beneath his sole.

From another shirt pocket, he removed a packet of freeze-dried fruit, shoving some into his mouth. Brittle, the particles slowly softened, releasing a stale but not unpleasant taste. Apricots or peaches—he couldn't tell which. But if he sucked on them patiently, they might last in his mouth for as long as thirty minutes. Remembering the dysentery that he'd suffered during his six-week struggle to reach the DMZ after he escaped from the prison camp, he wasn't about to trust the fruit that dangled in abundance from trees around him.

He kept going. Shapes loomed out of the morning mist, their slender coils alarming him till he came close enough to recognize them as harmless vines on branches above him.

Hearing movement behind him, he suddenly swung with his knife. In a single smooth deadly swoop, the blade whistling through the air, he struck his target, snicking, slicing as if through butter, and the suspended body of a decapitated writhing snake entwined upon itself, then sagged, let go, and flopped obscenely onto the ground.

He studied the viper's unblinking head, replaced his knife, and hurried on.

— 13 —

Five hours later, drenched with sweat, he scrambled, breathing hard, to the top of another rise, but here instead of facing another valley below, he followed a level trail through underbrush that gradually opened out to reveal a clearing on a plateau.

He paused to subdue the heaving of his chest. Sucking gritty sweat off his lips, he wiped it from his forehead and eyes, his vision blurry for a moment. As his eyes cleared, however, he still faced indistinct images, the mist from the night having been replaced by heat haze from the scorching sun directly above him.

He scanned the towering jumbled rain forest that encircled the clearing.

And blinked with religious awe at the enormous stone face, wreathed in vines, that loomed from the haze.

Walking slowly, respectfully forward, he realized where he was, distinguishing other objects in the undergrowth around the clearing.

It surprised and disturbed him. He'd entered the atrium of a long-abandoned wat. The ruins of a Buddhist temple. Several hundred years old. As he passed through the haze, other objects became discernible.

Serene despite the ravages of centuries, two stone Buddhas—massive, thirty feet tall—sat flanking the well-worn steps of a weathered temple. Trees and vines all but obscured the cracked and tumbled forms of ornately carved walls.

There were ghosts here, he thought.

Pausing in the center of the courtyard, he felt the majesty of the sky. Spirelike structures suggested themselves in the fog beyond.

He bowed his head in respect. His religious training had been complicated. Born of an Italian father and a Navajo mother, he'd been an altar boy at the Catholic church in Bowie, Arizona, and had as well been initiated into the sacred Indian rites at his mother's tribal village outside town. But though moved by both devotions, it had not been until his tours in Nam that he had chosen a religion for himself rather than the two which by the circumstances of his birth had been chosen for him.

If he'd been asked to declare his affiliation, he'd have described himself as a follower of Zen, a Buddhist. He'd acquired this persuasion because of a mountain tribesman with whom he'd worked on his first in-country mission.

Having endured the rigors of Special Forces training, having become among the elite, the best, he had still not survived his initiating test-under-fire. And though he hadn't chosen this war, hadn't enlisted and instead had been drafted—it was a measure of his inborn skill that Special Forces, which never took draftees, had agreed to accept him—he'd embraced his patriotic duty with determination and fervor. Wasn't that what you were supposed to do?

But training was one thing. Actual combat was another. He remembered a line from a book that he'd admired in his innocence—*Catch-22*—and its main character's sudden understanding about the ultimate secret of war. "Holy fuck, they're trying to kill me!" Having nearly frozen in a firefight against the Cong, bullets slicing the leaves around him, members of his A-team screaming and dying around him, his urine staining his pants, he'd felt the mountain tribesman grab him and drag him back to safety.

And because that tribesman had saved his life, that tribesman had no choice except with honor to acknowledge the profundity of their spiritual bond. Thus, from that tribesman, who showed no fear, Rambo had learned how he himself could not show fear. Because he didn't feel it. Zen. The ultimate weapon. What reason would he have to be afraid of death once he understood that death did not exist? That nothing existed. That life itself—this tree, this rock, this butterfly—was but an illusion. A veil. A magical trick that the Holy One played on us. And if you saw through the trick, if you learned the essential difference between illusion and what was real, which was the Holy One, then in passing through what the ignorant referred to as death, you entered the truly actual. You merged with the Holy One.

And achieved your destiny.

But if you took too much for granted, if you didn't respect the challenge of illusion that the Holy One had set for you, if you simply invited the mystery called death, then instead of merging with the Holy One, you might come back as a leech.

This powerful vision, this understanding of the unimportance of what we foolishly called life, had given Rambo strength. And sometimes he felt that Zen, more than his government's halfhearted commitment to the war, had been what caused the Viet Cong to win. Because the Cong had understood that years, even centuries, didn't matter. That the rivers, the rain forest, the bullets that pierced their throats or tore their skulls apart, weren't real. But during this present stage in their existence, they had to comply with the Holy One's wishes and *pretend* that the physical was real. But to an American, for whom Disneyland and Tastee-Freeze were examples of all that was real, the rain forest, the bullets, the Agent Orange were enough to drive you insane. "Christ, get me out of here!" And so with the echo of Jim Morrison and the Doors reverberating in the nation's consciousness, America had left and lost.

But Rambo had survived.

Surveying the wat, he felt his heart seem to shrink with overwhelming respect and reverence. Zen. The religion that seemed the most powerful to him.

The most practical.

Because of what he did.

Because of what he was.

In the killing fields of combat, a Catholic might lose his soul. Even a Navajo.

But not a Buddhist.

Shifting toward the shadows of the overgrown temple, creeping noiselessly, he stiffened, hearing someone else make a noise.

His senses alert, he lunged toward bushes, drew his pistol, and crouched in a firing position.

To his left, a figure crept through the rain forest, barely moving the foliage. He shifted his aim. The presence stopped. He stopped his arm and aimed steadily.

He saw clothing now. A black pajama uniform. Viet Cong. The soldier moved forward. Rambo tracked with him, his finger tensing on the powerful pistol's trigger.

But what if this soldier wasn't alone? The Colt's report

would draw the others toward him.

No. He knew a better way.

He entered the undergrowth, ducking gracefully, silently through the foliage, making no noise.

His quarry did the same.

Now Rambo saw the distinctive silhouette of an AK-47. Close, closer, one with the bushes, he lunged, grabbing the enemy's chin, slashing his knife toward the enemy's throat, and as his blade was about to slice, the enemy's wide straw hat fell off. Long, lush, sheeny black hair tumbled down.

A micro-inch from the smooth curved throat, he froze.

"Let me go!" The voice was Vietnamese.

And female.

The woman, a native, seemed in her late twenties. Small. Deceptively delicate. Gorgeous as almost every young Vietnamese woman was. With the elegance of an Oriental vase. Her eyes were wide open, expressive. Her mouth was strong, sensuous, parted in sudden fear.

She spoke again in Vietnamese, repeating, "Let me go!" Her voice lowered as she humbly cast her eyes down. "Please." She raised her eyes. Apparently realizing that Rambo, despite his camouflage makeup, was American, she surprisingly switched to English. "I sorry. I did not expect. You first tourist here in long time. Did not mean to interrupt."

His knife still ready, Rambo kept staring.

"You come here see Buddha, ask for truth?" she asked.

He still didn't speak.

"Or you just lost? If so, I guide you."

Rambo used Vietnamese. "No, I'm not lost. Just looking for someone."

She smiled at his fluent idiom and switched back to Vietnamese. "Someone called maybe 'Night Orchid'?"

Again in her language, he said, "That was one of the names I was given."

"Another was Co Phuong Bao?"

He felt foolish. Not because he'd almost killed her. That had been merely prudent.

No, he felt foolish because when he'd first heard that his contact's name was Co, he'd automatically translated it into English.

And Co meant virgin.

"Do you understand my name in English?" she asked.

He nodded.

"My mother was a comedian." She frowned. "Are you the one they sent? Rambo?"

Again he nodded. "Another second and I would have killed—"

"I was hiding. You didn't come on time. I thought you were one of the mercenaries still here. Why are you late?"

"Well, I had some problems. I got hung up."

They faced each other awkwardly.

"I see it in your eyes," she said. "You didn't expect a woman."

He shrugged.

"Does that make a difference?" she asked.

He shook his head. "In America, they've got something called the women's liberation movement."

"Sounds Communist."

He grinned and shook his head. "It's kind of complicated, but what it means is that it's not what sex you are but how well you do what you do that's important."

"Then you don't need to worry." She stopped speaking Vietnamese. "I need to practice. Better speak English, yes?"

He had to smile. "Yes. You speak it well."

"You betcha."

"Where'd you learn?"

"In the old days. University of Saigon."

Which made her not twenty-eight or so, but in her early thirties.

She raised her chin proudly. "Have master's degree in economics." And looked disappointed. "Not use too much now. The Communists in charge. Hey, you got time? You want some food?"

He chuckled. "Sure. What have you got?"

Co reached behind her and unslung a canvas food tube

from her back. He recognized the tube's design. He'd seen it on many dead Viet Cong.

She pulled its cap off proudly. "What have I got? *Nuac nam.*"

His stomach rumbled.

She unrolled several rubber-tree leaves, revealing compacted rice soaked in a sauce that made his nostrils flare from its pungency.

He accepted one opened leaf along with the chopsticks she offered. And with skills that he hadn't used in years, he shoveled the rice to his mouth.

"Have you really got a master's degree?" he asked in English, chewing, swallowing.

"Sure." She grinned. "I only sound like a four-year-old in *your* language."

He laughed again and shoved more rice to his mouth. "Mmm. What's this sauce?"

"Fermented fish."

"Yeah, I remember now." Its pungent taste clung like oil to his tongue. And not knowing why, he laughed yet again, cramming more rice in his mouth.

Across from him, the Buddha loomed.

— 14 —

As they moved through the tangle of the rain forest, veering back and forth past obstructions, Rambo studied her. Slender, a head shorter than himself, her figure concealed by her loose black pajamas, she slipped past trees, through undergrowth, with fluid grace. He admired the prudence with which she avoided trails, the skill with which she found passages where there didn't seem to be any.

She'd asked if it bothered him that she was a woman, and his answer had been the truth. As long as she did her job well, it made no difference to him what sex she was.

And indeed sexual attraction itself would not be an issue.

When he'd gone back to the States from Nam, he'd been shocked to learn the attitude that many Americans, especially college students who'd demonstrated against the war, had toward returning vets. Mass murderers. Baby killers. One of the names he'd been most often called was "rapist." He'd been baffled as much as appalled. The assumption behind such an accusation was that killing made you so blood-crazed that you'd commit atrocities of any kind.

Rapist? The crime was repugnant to him. It was true that he'd heard about soldiers who'd raped Vietnamese women in villages after an attack. But those men had been treated with contempt by fellow soldiers. Lowlife—animals who'd been that way in the world and hadn't changed when they'd come to Nam. But as for the soldiers whom Rambo had known and respected . . .

Didn't civilians understand that combat turned you away from sex? Never mind rape, the thought of which he loathed. Combat turned you away from *normal* sex. *Consenting* sex.

Growing up, a teen-ager in Bowie, Arizona, he'd been as interested in girls as any other hormone-inspired boy he went to school with. Of course, in those days the so-called sexual revolution had not yet occurred, and he'd stayed a virgin till he was twenty-one, his partner the girl he planned to marry. He still remembered her lovely straw-blond hair. But then he'd gone into the army, and when he came back from the war, she'd already married someone else, had two young sons and a daughter, and spoke to him as if they'd never been more than casual friends. Indeed, she seemed embarrassed, as if she didn't want to remember him at all.

He didn't resent that she'd married someone else. After all, he'd been gone a long time and for a while had been given up for dead. He couldn't have expected her to wait for him.

But the truth was, he felt relieved.

Because marriage now seemed impossible for him.

And having children?

Unthinkable.

Because, after the horrors he'd endured, sex had ceased to be an urge. He couldn't bear even the thought of getting that close to someone. Not just emotionally. Literally. Physically. His stomach would clench, his skin would turn clammy.

Not that he was impotent. Not at all. He sometimes had wet dreams. On occasion, rarely, he masturbated.

But intercourse was out of the question.

Because when you got that near to someone you were unprotected, vulnerable.

Because during sex you lost control.

Because even with contraception there was always the chance that a child would be conceived.

And a child didn't deserve the anguish of being born into such a terrible world, a world in which wars and prison camps were not only possible but commonplace for too many people.

For himself.

As he continued shifting through the undergrowth, watching her skillfully lead the way, he thought once more about her question. Did it make a difference that she was a woman?

No.

— 15 —

They emerged from bushes to the sloping bank of a muddy narrow river. On Rambo's map, it was called the Ca.

Pausing, he studied its sluggish current. "How do we head north from here?" He used English, remembering that she wanted to practice.

"I have arranged . . ."—she thought a moment, choosing her words—". . . transportation. Old routes not safe." Her eyes became troubled. "But when we reach upriver, I think you feel disappointed."

"Oh? Why's that?"

She shook her head. "I go up to this camp two months ago. Nobody there. Empty for years."

"But . . ." Rambo frowned. "Why would they send us to a deserted camp?"

"Maybe the soldiers come back since two months ago."

"Maybe. As long as they brought the prisoners with them."

"This way." Co pointed to the left, upriver. "Transportation not far."

— 16 —

He heard them as he stepped from the forest. Ahead, in a brackish inlet, he saw a crudely fashioned hut made from corrugated metal and bamboo walls. It was perched above the river, supported by skeletal tree roots that projected from the bank. A platform stuck out over the water, and on it, two grotesque filthy Orientals, one wearing earrings and a sweaty cowboy hat, the other an ammunition belt across an elbowless tuxedo jacket, cursed drunkenly at each other in Vietnamese while they struggled for control of a bottle.

As Rambo came closer, he recognized the label on the bottle.

Budweiser.

Co shouted to them in Vietnamese. "Let's go!"

The men turned abruptly. Startled, they grabbed for their AK-47's, dropping the bottle, no longer caring that it rolled off the platform, splashing into the water.

Surly, they aimed.

Then through their red bleery eyes, they apparently recognized Co. One muttered to the other. The second man snorted.

And Rambo relaxed as they lowered their weapons. But he heard the brush of leaves behind him and turned, distressed as two other river rats emerged from concealment in the forest.

"These guys look like they'd sell their mothers," he murmured to Co in English.

"Sometimes they do. They are pirates. Opium runners."

She tried to sound optimistic. "But best way upriver. Not get army suspicious."

"Right now, it isn't the army I'm worried about."

Next to the hut, a delapidated sampan wallowed in the water, its deck housing, too, made from corrugated metal and bamboo. From its cabin, an even more grotesque Oriental came out and stepped onto the shore, slightly weaving as he approached. He had long greasy hair, an assortment of cheap necklaces dangling down his chest, four wristwatches along one arm, and a pearl-handled revolver stuck into the waist of oil-stained American designer jeans a size too large for him. He grinned, revealing bare gums where his upper front teeth should have been.

"Co, keep using English when you talk to me," Rambo said, his voice low, before the man arrived.

She seemed confused, but she did what he asked, gesturing toward the man, bowing politely. "This is Captain Trong Kinh."

Rambo bowed as well. "Captain."

Kinh showed more of his gums. Tapping his chest, he spoke in English. "Wa-ky number one. You come number one sampan."

"Yes, I can see that," Rambo said. "And I thank you for helping me."

"Plenty glad to help, you bet." Kinh seemed fascinated by the two quivers slung across Rambo's back.

"You speak my language well."

"But do you speak mine?" the captain asked, switching to Vietnamese.

With apparent confusion, Rambo glanced from the captain to Co.

Still using Vietnamese, Kinh turned to Co. "He does not understand?"

She shook her head.

Kinh's toothless grin dissolved. "You brought the money?"

"Here." Co reached inside her pajamas and handed him a wad of crumpled American money.

Kinh greedily counted it. He squinted. "Where's the rest?"

"Half now, half later."

"That wasn't the deal."

Co simply stared at him.

Kinh's lips curled. He swung toward his men, barking orders.

They scrambled drunkenly to obey, shouting contradictory commands at each other, clumsily casting off mooring lines from the sampan, jumping aboard, one nearly losing his balance, flailing his arms to keep from falling into the water. The others jeered, hooting obscene insults.

As if a button had been pushed, Kinh's hideous toothless grin returned. He gestured toward the sampan.

Reluctant, walking with Co, Rambo got on.

— 17 —

In the cabin, a raisin-faced Vietnamese woman holding an infant shuffled aside as Rambo entered. The room was shadowy, smoky, its roof so low that he had to stoop.

It was also claustrophobically cluttered. Every possible space was crammed with scavenged or looted junk. Empty Coca-Cola cases, rust-pitted hubcaps, an old Victrola radio, a TV set with a broken screen, mildewed books, dead chickens, an ice-cube tray, a tireless bicycle wheel, two outboard motors. There seemed no pattern or logic to it.

But behind ammo cases, Rambo saw the upright barrels of several rifles and shotguns.

Three members of the crew stumbled in, adding to the crowded stench in the cabin. One of them produced a bottle of Jim Beam whiskey, drinking from it only to have it yanked from his hand. The winkled woman with the infant lit a long-stemmed clay pipe. As the smoke reached Rambo, his nostrils twitched from the sick-sweet odor of opium.

He felt the sampan list as it drifted from shore and started upriver. An engine sputtered weakly.

Kinh's shadow appeared in the open doorway. Wiping saliva from his lips as it leaked past his toothless gums, he used English again. "You want a drink?" He gestured toward the whiskey bottle one of his men was drinking from.

Rambo shook his head.

"Too bad." Kinh brightened. "No, not too bad. More for me." He grabbed the bottle from the man and cursed him.

"Sleep here," Co told Rambo. "Safe while we go upriver."

"Sleep?" Rambo glanced at the clutter. "Where? And what about patrol boats?"

"Ah." Kinh waggled his finger. "No worry patrol boats." Like a kid unwrapping a Christmas present, he raised the lid on a greasy wooden locker, peering delightedly inside.

Rambo understood his delight when he saw what Kinh took out of the locker.

The pride of his arsenal. A huge forbidding Russian-made RPG-7 portable rocket launcher.

Kinh's eyes glistened evilly. "We will have no problems."

"No," Rambo said. "No problems."

– 4 –

THE COMPOUND

— 1 —

Trautman stared out the huge open door of the hangar, his muscles aching tensely as the sun dipped slowly lower. He'd been waiting, watching it, for several hours. Before that, he'd been pacing the hangar. And before that, he'd been standing behind the radio operator, concentrating on the instrument panel as if by sheer intensity he could make Rambo's voice interrupt the static.

Yes, wait.

That was all he could do.

And pray.

But this much he took hope from. If anyone could have survived that disastrous bailout last night, it was Rambo.

Sure.

Then, dammit, Trautman thought, why hasn't he called in? I never thought I'd see the day I actually hoped for one of my men in-country to have his radio broken.

Turning, he straightened expectantly as Murdock walked over. "Anything?"

Murdock just shook his head.

"It's not in my nature."

"What?"

"To be a fifth wheel," Trautman said. "I want to fly out with the extraction team tonight."

"I don't think that's necessary."

"It might not be necessary. The point is, I want to go."

"Permission denied."

Trautman bristled. *"Denied?"*

"Too dangerous. That'll be a pretty hairy ride. Full colonels aren't supposed to risk their lives. You've paid your dues. You've earned the right to avoid exposing yourself."

"Why don't you let *me* worry about the risk? I said I want to—"

"No, this is everybody's worry. *My* worry," Murdock said. "I don't need a full colonel to get himself shot down over Vietnam. Correct me if I'm wrong, but you're here as a courtesy." Murdock raised his hands. "And yes, I'll admit it—to keep your 'boy,' as you call him, under control. But as long as you're here, you're a part of the team. And I say, all things considered, I don't want you taking unnecessary risks. As it is, I'm not even sure I ought to let Ericson take the extraction chopper in."

"Wait a minute. You're not talking about . . . ? Abort the mission?"

"I'm tempted, believe me. This is getting more dicey than I planned."

"But you gave your word. You said the chopper would be there, and dammit, it will be. You have to keep to the schedule."

"Gave my word? To who? Rambo? We don't even know he's alive. The odds are against it."

"No," Trautman said. "You gave your word to *me*. And by God, I intend to make you keep your promise."

Murdock considered him. "It's like that, huh?"

"Yeah," Trautman said, "like that."

"All right, I see where you're coming from. And I sure as hell don't want any dissenting reports when we pack in this operation. You want me to go through with this and send in Ericson with the chopper? Fine. You want to risk your ass by going in with him? That's fine, too. It's no skin off mine. But Colonel . . ."

"What?"

"I have to give you credit. You sure are loyal."

— 2 —

Rambo stood inside the open door to the sampan's cabin, concealed by a canvas sheet, peering through a gap toward the setting sun that reflected coppery off the river. From the rear, the ancient outboard motor stubbornly continued to sputter. As the sampan moved slowly upriver, he watched the traffic it passed. Smaller, hand-powered sampans guided by silhouetted boatmen in broad conical straw hats. Occasional large motor-driven sampans like this one. He passed a peaceful village—rows of hootches marching up the hill on stilts, brown children splashing naked, happy, into the water, their squeals of laughter echoing across the river. Then the broad expanse of the forest returned, and he realized that except for the sound of the motor this scene would have been the same a hundred years ago. Or five hundred years ago.

Wars had come and gone. Regimes and ideologies had ebbed and flowed. But what remained were the land and the people.

And when you came right down to it, what people wanted wasn't politics but to be left alone.

He closed the gap in the canvas sheet that concealed him at the door and glanced at Co, hunched against an ammo box, asleep.

Her face was serene.

And childlike.

And beautiful.

Her eyes flickered. Gradually awakening, she noticed him and smiled.

"You not sleepy?" she asked in English.

"Later," he said. "When this is over."

"I think it never over."

"You're right about that."

Two members of the crew were still inside. Sprawling drunkenly on crates, they glanced at each other, puzzled by the unfamiliar language they heard.

"We eat again, yes?" Co asked.

"If you want, we eat again."

She opened one of the rubber-tree leaves and offered him chopsticks.

Sometimes hers brushed against his as they reached for the remnants of fermented fish and rice.

"You're welcome," she said.

He reddened. "I'm sorry. Out here, I forget my manners."

"I know. I make a joke."

He grinned.

"How they get you into this?" she asked.

"Long story."

"And this," she said, "long ride."

He shook his head, chewing rice. "Not long enough to explain." He swallowed. "Hey, what about you? What got you started working for spooks?"

"Spooks?"

"Intelligence work. What you're doing now."

"Oh. Yes, I see. Spooks. Very good." Meditating, she sucked on her chopsticks. "They talk to me at university before fall of Saigon. Make deal."

"Yeah, that's what the spooks are good at," Rambo said, remembering the quarry, the ache in his muscles, the sweat on his back. "Making deals."

"My brother captain in Communist army. Need papers to go United States or North Vietnamese will execute. Yes, spooks make deal. He go. I stay here, do work for them. My brother and my son, they also go United States."

Rambo stopped chewing, surprised. "Your son?"

Co's eyes dropped. "Nguyen. He twelve now. Not see him for eight years. I bet he big. Maybe not big as American boy. But strong."

"Yes, strong." Rambo swallowed painfully. "In America, with lots of food, I know he is. What about his father?"

Co shrugged, a stoic acceptance that he'd learned to expect from Vietnamese. "Dead. Killed in war."

Sure, Rambo thought, she'd seen death in every form it could take. She expected it as a common element in everyday life. "I'm sorry."

"Yes." She hesitated, and Rambo remembered how bigoted Americans had insisted that killing a gook wasn't the same as the gooks killing an American. ("See, those fucking Orientals, they don't respect life like we do. Look at the shitty buildings they're crowded into. Life is cheap over there." Americans, Rambo thought. Always assuming that the rest of the world had the same high standard of living.) "Yes," Co said, her voice tight, "I was sorry, too. I think about him. Many nights."

He allowed her a graceful way to avoid the indignity of exposing her grief, changing the subject. "And what about your son? Nguyen? Is that what you said his name was? Where did he go in the States? What city?"

She proudly announced, "Huntington Beach, California."

"Yeah." Rambo considered. "It's nice there. He's probably even got a surfboard."

"Surfboard?"

"A piece of wood you stand on to ride a wave."

"Ride a—?"

"It's sort of hard to describe. You have to see it to believe it. What I meant was, your son, I bet he's probably breaking girls' hearts."

Co became indignant. "Nguyen is *good* boy."

"Sure." Rambo laughed. "Of course he is."

"He safe. What matters. Not like here. Not like his father." Co set down her chopsticks, her eyes bleak. "Too much death. Death everywhere. I just..."

"Yes?"

"Want to live."

So you made a bargain with the spooks to risk your life in exchange for keeping your son safe, Rambo thought. You're a damned fine lady.

"And what about you?" Co asked.

"I'm not sure what you . . ."

"What do *you* want?"

"Me?" He shrugged. "To survive."

"Survive? That different from living."

"I guess it is. I don't think I've lived since . . ."

"Not so easy . . . even . . . to survive here. Still war here."

"Well," Rambo said, "to survive war, you have to . . ."

"Yes?"

". . . become war."

Co raised her eyebrows, puzzled. "Then why spooks pick you? Because you like to fight?"

Rambo shook his head. "Because I'm good at it . . . and because I'm expendable."

"Ex-pend-a-ble?"

"Know what it means?"

"Don't tell me. . . . It mean if you in crowd in car . . . and car have accident . . . and you the only one die . . . no one care. Yes?"

"You got it."

Rambo glanced at a leather thong around her neck. As she leaned forward, a medallion attached to it had dangled from the top of her pajamas. He touched it.

A tiny golden Buddha.

"It bring me good luck," Co said, glancing from his fingers up to his face. "What bring *you* good luck?"

He pulled his fingers back from the tiny Buddha, debating.

And lowered them, clasping the butt of his knife. He shifted his eyes toward the lounging pirates.

Co understood.

— 3 —

Frantic shouts outside made him stiffen.

Drawing the knife, he spun toward the canvas across the door. In contrast with the sampan's sputtering outboard motor, a powerful roaring engine—louder with every second—sped closer.

Co raced to the curtain, peered out, and swung toward him. "Army! River patrol!"

His stomach contracted, terribly cold.

The drunken pirates tried to rouse themselves. Muttering, they lurched toward the canvas.

But Rambo was already diving toward a tarpaulin that drooped across a crate. He scrambled behind the crate, pulling the tarp over him, its must overwhelming, feeling clutter crash down on him, confused only for a moment till he realized that Co was burying him.

He clutched his knife.

And drew his pistol, releasing the safety catch.

He breathed as slightly as he could, frantic not to disturb the motionless tarp.

— 4 —

Co toppled the final pile of clutter over him, a bicycle pump landing on a stringless guitar and the roller off an old washing machine. Her heart pounding, she heard the powerful roar of the patrol boat's engine speed so close that the metal walls of the cabin rattled. It seemed to be right outside.

She glanced toward her rifle but didn't have time to reach the weapon before the curtain was jerked aside.

Kinh rushed in.

His bloodshot eyes looked fierce as he threw open the greasy wooden locker, yanked out the rocket launcher, and slammed a projectile into its tube.

Co stopped him. In Vietnamese, she said, "Try to use it. I'll aim it toward your root."

Kinh stared.

"Which is what you think with instead of your brain."

Glaring, he balanced his pride against her wisdom. "You've got a better way?"

"Greed." She yanked a packet of North Vietnamese bills from inside her pajamas and pressed them into his hand. "Go ahead. Do what you're good at."

His thoughts jelled sluggishly. But all at once the compliment amused him. He showed his toothless gums again. "Why not?"

And stooped to leave the cabin.

Co followed. On the deck of the sampan, shielding her eyes against the sunset reflecting off the water, she saw the massive roaring patrol boat pull up in an arc, its huge wave almost swamping the sampan. As the deck tilted one way, then the other, she pressed a hand against the metal wall of the cabin, keeping her balance, and glanced up with pretended innocence at the patrol boat above her.

Its powerful engine suddenly stopped, the unnerving stillness worse than the roar. Afterwaves sloshed the bow. Six grim-lipped soldiers on deck wore the uniforms of the North Vietnamese Navy. At the bow, a deck gunner racked back the bolt on his R.P.K. machine gun and swiveled it down toward the sampan, aiming, ready to fire. Wary, the others held AK-47's. The patrol boat's captain, large-chested, arrogant, raised a loud hailer to his mouth. His voice was sharp, metallic, booming, as he blurted rapid orders in Vietnamese. "Stand ready! Stay as you are! Prepare to be boarded!"

Kinh's river rats shuffled awkwardly on deck, looking— if possible—even more stupid. The scrawny raisin-faced woman fed her gaunt sickly child from a sagging breast.

Kinh gestured magnanimously, his necklaces tinkling. "Hey, of course. Come on. We got nothing to hide. Say, you want a drink?"

The patrol boat's captain twitched his nostrils. As a guard stood on each side of him, each aiming a submachine gun, he drew his pistol, tapped its barrel on the palm of his other hand, and jumped down onto the sampan. His knees bending, he quickly straightened, catching his balance, self-consciously keeping his dignity. He glanced suspiciously around.

Co stood outside the entrance to the cabin, trying to look impressed by his uniform.

The patrol boat captain muttered, shoved her out of his way, and stalked inside the cabin.

Kinh followed. "Or maybe you want a watch? Good watch. American."

As the sun dipped halfway below the forested horizon, Co squinted through the doorway, trying to pierce the shadows in there.

The patrol boat captain poked and kicked at the clutter. "What kind of watch?"

"A Bulova."

"Give it to me." He jabbed at the junk on the canvas sheet that covered Rambo. "You mentioned a drink."

"Good whiskey." Kinh opened a crate and gave him an unopened bottle of Cutty Sark.

"Where'd you get this junk?"

"People lose it along the river."

"I thought you said you had nothing to hide."

"Does this look like it's hidden?"

"And what about those guns over there?"

"What guns? Oh, *those* guns. Why, we need them for our protection. You wouldn't believe how many thieves are on the river these days."

"Oh, I believe it, all right."

"Of course. You probably have to defend yourself against thieves every day."

"For the good of the people. And when I find thieves, I like to give them what they've got coming."

"I'm sure you're overworked. With not enough pay. People don't appreciate how much the navy does for them."

The patrol boat captain kicked at the locker that contained the rocket launcher. "That's always the way. In the navy, you learn to expect no appreciation. No one shows gratitude for our protection."

"Perhaps this will show how grateful we are." Kinh pulled out the wad of money Co had given him.

The patrol boat captain licked his finger, thumbing through the bills, counting. "Only this much appreciation?"

"Ah, but I was just reaching for my other pocket." Kinh gave him another wad of bills.

"Yes. Now I can see how grateful you are for the job we do. And in return"—the patrol boat captain glanced around— "let me give you a word of warning. Be careful. I'm told there aren't only thieves out there but smugglers, too."

"Vile vicious degenerates." Kinh spat on the floor. "Their mothers curse the day they gave birth."

"Perhaps we'll meet again." With another sharp kick at the locker that contained the rocket launcher, the captain stalked toward the doorway.

"Oh, I look forward to it," Kinh said.

Co pivoted out of the captain's way just in time. He stopped on the deck, scowled at Kinh's scummy-looking crew, and climbed up onto the patrol boat.

Restraining her tension, Co watched as the captain gestured abruptly. The patrol boat roared. It surged away, making the sampan list again.

As soon as she couldn't see it anymore—its engine droning farther away past a bend in the river—she ducked inside the cabin.

"How you doing, Rambo?"

Past the crate, she saw a shadow move. Squirming, dumping the cluttered objects off him, Rambo rose like a spectre from beneath the canvas, his knife in one hand, his pistol in the other.

"I'd sooner be in Philadelphia."

"What? I not understand. Why Philadelphia?"

"An old joke. W. C. Fields."

"Yes. Joke. W. C. Fields." And though she still didn't understand it, she grinned.

— 5 —

It was night. Earlier it had rained. Now moonlight made the forest seem alive with reflections glistening off leaves. Everywhere water dripped. They climbed slippery tree roots up a steep embankment. Hunching low to conceal their silhouettes at the top, they quickly chose a route down the other side.

"Wait here," Co had told Kinh after they'd slipped from the sampan, standing knee-deep in muddy water. "We come back, pay rest."

Kinh had been displeased, not wanting to risk a challenge from another patrol boat. But greed had been more important than his nerves.

The thing is, can he be trusted? Rambo thought, shifting through darkness down the slope. Suppose Kinh changes his mind and decides the money isn't worth it? What if when we get back he isn't there?

Then we'll just have to find another way downriver. That's all, Rambo thought.

But something else occurred to him. If Kinh planned to leave them here, it was logical to assume that Kinh would also have tried to take their money, all of it, and kill them. Eight pirates against the two of us. Kinh might have guessed that the odds were in his favor. For that matter, he might just as well have tried to kill us back at his hut. Why go to all the bother of bringing us up here if he didn't intend to keep his bargain?

No, the more Rambo thought about it, the more he felt confident that Kinh would be back there waiting for them.

As he reached the dark bottom of the slope, his boot touched something round and hollow. It rolled and clacked against something else.

Next to him, he heard Co step on something that rattled.

He paused and frowned. Booby traps?

Then we should have been blown to pieces.

Gourds?

They sounded too brittle to be gourds.

He took another step and froze again when he heard the scrape of stripped dead branches, jumbled in a pile. When he tried to step around them, he discovered that the pile extended in this direction for quite a distance. In fact, whatever was down here, he realized he was surrounded by it.

What the—?

His eyes adjusted to the greater blackness down here, straining to take advantage of the subtle moonlight that managed to filter down this far.

He began to see white round objects. But many more ivory long ones, some of them curved. Heaped, intersecting in no discernible pattern.

But then the pattern *was* discernible, and reflexive bile rose bitter hot into his mouth.

He was staring at bones. *Human* bones. Skulls and skeletons crammed on top of each other, meshed together, vines growing in and out of shattered rib cages, tendrils protruding from fleshless mouths and eyeless sockets.

But the mouths had teeth, and that told him everything. Out here, deep in the forest, barely existing on a meager diet, the Vietnamese didn't keep their teeth. Most adults gummed their food instead of chewing it.

No, these skeletons, these skulls (larger than those of most Vietnamese), were Caucasian.

Were . . .

American?

Dear God, he thought as his spine shivered despite the sultry humidity, this is what the soldiers did with the prisoners who died. Instead of burying the bodies . . .

Surely not. He swallowed more bile.

. . . they dragged them out here and simply tossed them into the ravine. The rain forest would quickly do the work that the death crew had avoided. Animals, insects, microbes would ravage the bodies, strip the flesh. Scavengers would gnaw and scatter the bones. The danger of disease would be minimal. And the stench of death wouldn't rise above the ravine. It would soon disperse completely when the rain forest had finished its work.

He glanced toward Co, faintly able to see the expression on her shadowy face. An expression of horror. Of shock.

He tapped her shoulder and pointed toward the opposite slope.

She hesitated. Inhaling deeply, she nodded.

Making as little noise as possible, they waded through the charnel pit. Skeletons clicked as he stepped among them. Rats scrambled toward deeper sections of the piles.

And after seconds that seemed torturous minutes, he reached the brush-covered bank on the other side.

But though he should have felt relieved as he started climbing again, he instead felt apprehensive. Not because he knew that the compound was close now, that violence probably lurked ahead. Quite the opposite. He felt apprehensive because the thought of death's stench had made him realize that there *wasn't* any stench here. These bodies had been stripped clean long ago. At the wat, Co had told him that she'd studied this camp two months before and it had been empty.

Maybe it was *still* empty. Maybe he wouldn't find any prisoners. Maybe he'd come here for nothing.

— 6 —

He reached yet another rise, but before he could duck through underbrush, Co stopped him. Up here, the moonlight more vivid, he saw the tension on her face. She glanced distressed ahead of him.

He understood.

His muscles hardened. With a tight-lipped nod, he sank to the loamy ground, its smell so rich that it was stifling, and began to crawl past leaves, through ferns.

Parted a branch.

And saw the prison camp.

Below, across from him, spread out in shadows, it filled — a wide, long ravine. But this ravine, unlike the one he'd just left, didn't stretch from his right to left. Instead, it went straight ahead of him. And it was wide.

He'd never seen the camp from this perspective, but he couldn't fail to recognize it. His six months here had branded it into his mind. And his nightmares seared it there even more. It was hell on earth. The slime pit, the torture racks, the bamboo cages so short and small that you couldn't stand and couldn't sit, the pain in your haunches from bending your knees, the agony in the back of your neck from keeping your chin pressed against your chest . . . You thought you'd go crazy. But you knew that if you did you'd never survive. You were sure that any second now your will would snap and you'd scream, shriek, wail with absolute hopelessness, torment, despair. But you wouldn't. You'd control yourself for just another second, and then another second after that, and you'd think about camping in the desert in Arizona, going through every motion in your head, pitching the tent, making a fire, cooking beef stew that you poured from a can, tasting its thick tangy gravy. Or you'd think about racing your battered souped-up Ford down a back-country road, raising dust behind you, feeling the jolt of bumps as you whooped and revved it all the way up to a hundred and ten.

But then you'd realize that no matter how many mind games you tried, you were still in the cage or down in the pit or on the rack, your hands tied above you, your shoulders slowly pulling from their sockets as your feet dangled.

And then you'd remember your mountain tribesman friend and know that camping in the desert didn't matter. And racing your Ford didn't matter.

Nothing mattered.

Except for the way of Zen.

Because nothing was real.

Not the cage. Not the pit. Not the rack.

All was illusion. There wasn't any pain. How could there be pain if he didn't have a body?

Only a mind. And staring at a nub on the bamboo of the cage before him (the bamboo wasn't real, the nub wasn't real), he focused on a mosquito that perched on the nub, and focused on the wings of that mosquito (the mosquito wasn't real, its wings weren't real), and transported himself into a speck within God's eye (but God was real).

And survived.

Now remembering, staring at the camp, he shuddered. Logically, he knew, he should have been able to follow his attitude to the limit and believe that the camp itself wasn't real.

But he wasn't able to do that, perhaps because Zen for him was more a defense mechanism than a philosophy. Or perhaps because to believe that the camp wasn't real would force him to believe that any Americans held prisoner there weren't real either. And with all his soul, he rebeled against that thought.

The torment in him seemed pointless at the moment.

For true to Co's prediction, the camp was totally dark, seemingly deserted.

On each side, guard towers had been strategically arranged. Their designers had taken advantage of a tall tree on each side of the camp and used the trunks for supports, establishing the sentinel boxes within the upper spreading branches. Good camouflage. A judicious reliance on at-site materials. Barbed wire was strung along a series of wooden posts that formed a rough square to enclose the compound. Another sequence of barbed wire formed a second barrier, but this wire had merely been unrolled instead of anchored, its Slinky-toy appearance zigzagged at random.

The entrance to the compound was directly below him— a large wooden gate with a sentry box to the right. Again at-site materials had been used—the back of the box was the wide trunk of a tree. A dirt trail led past the box, through the gate, toward three wooden barracks arranged in a U.

The bottom of the U faced Rambo. The open end faced a large grottolike opening in a cliff.

The entire hellish arrangement was totally different from the way Rambo had heard prison camps described in the States. Preconceptions, probably due to depictions of prison camps in World War II, made most Americans think of bright open areas, no cover for a hundred yards around.

But this one was cramped by the forested cliffs on each side, and even in daylight, the camp had felt gloomy and dark.

Sometimes, Rambo knew, when you left a place and had things happen to you and then came back to that place, you found that your memory no longer matched what you saw. Certainly he'd felt that way when he returned—briefly— to what he thought was his home in Bowie, Arizona. Here in the prison camp, remembered images of Bowie had magnified gloriously in his mind, and when he went back to it, he discovered that his hometown was actually wretched, dismal, small. Or maybe he just didn't belong there anymore.

Belong anywhere.

But the compound below him, even from this new perspective, was exactly the same. Hell apparently was constant. His nightmare, once again before him instead of in his mind, hadn't changed.

He shuddered a second time, but from nervous energy now. He had his work to do.

"I told you. Looks empty," Co whispered, spread flat beside him in the undergrowth.

He studied one guard tower, then the other. No sign of a sentry.

"Move closer, yes?" Co whispered.

She rose to a crouch and began to creep forward.

Rambo grabbed her pajama leg.

She turned, her eyebrows raised in question.

Rambo pointed ahead of her. The taut wire, damp with humidity, glistened slightly in the moonlight. He gestured to her left—toward the Claymore mine attached to a tree. At the least, when she tripped the wire, her legs would have been blown away. More likely the bottom half of her body.

She scuttled back to him.

His gaze returned to the compound. A sudden brief glow, no longer than an instant, flicked on and off in the sentry box next to the gate.

Someone lighting a cigarette, Rambo guessed.

His instincts quickened.

Co had seen it, too. She turned to him in amazement, her mouth coming open.

He put a finger on her lips.

Because the stillness was broken by a burping, sputtering, almost farting engine drawing near. A headlight angled through the rain forest below, piercing the gloom.

Rambo strained to see beyond it.

A young woman, dressed in colorful but less than elegant clothes, steered a Lambretta scooter up to the entry shack. She stopped, the motor backfiring like a shot.

The ravine amplified sounds. Muffled but distinct, voices drifted up, the woman laughing, greeting the guard, the male sounding testy, surly.

Evidently unsure if Rambo understood, Co whispered, "Cyclo-girl whore from village. Business she say slow there."

Up here, with nothing to cause an echo, it was probably safe to risk a few barely audible words.

But Rambo again put his finger on her lips. Because her explanation wasn't necessary. Though he missed a few remarks, he got the gist of what the whore and the sentry said.

The sentry was being offered a deal. A *very* good deal.

But the sentry's testy voice made it seem as if *he* was offering the deal.

The sentry opened the gate to let the girl and her cycle through. "Remember," he said in Vietnamese. "In half an hour." And then he crudely said what he wanted to do with her.

But the cycle was already sputtering toward the huts.

Rambo's stomach contracted. In a smooth but urgent motion, he slipped the two quivers from his back. He pulled off their caps and with respect—indeed, with almost religious reverence—slid out the objects they contained, beginning to assemble them.

They looked so unusual that Co was forced to whisper, "What is it?"

— 7 —

The arrows. The bow.

Because of his half-Navajo ancestry, Rambo had learned early to be an expert archer. The rifle had replaced the bow as the primary hunting weapon in his mother's village, but many Navajos had still been proficient with it, and the oldest wisest man in the village had been his instructor, teaching him that strength was important, yes, but skill and endurance were *more* important, and concentration was the most important of all. To prove his statement, the old man—who often needed a cane to walk and sometimes had difficulty standing up—had drawn back the string on a bow that Rambo, even later as a muscular teen-ager, hadn't been able to draw. And the old man had released the arrow—thrum!—striking the bull's-eye of a target thirty yards away. Rambo's eyes had widened. "Because the mind draws the bow, not the body," the old man had said. "If your mind is strong, your body will obey. The archer is a medicine man. A priest in your other religion. To draw the bow is to go inward, to shut out the world, all distraction, to confront your spirit."

Rambo hadn't understood, of course. He was far too young, the old man said. But the sense of spirit would come. And Rambo tried to understand. He did. But his arrows seldom struck their target. "Because you're impatient," the old man said. "You worry. You try too hard. You must learn to love the bow, to guide the arrow with your spirit."

And one day, after great frustration, after months of trying without success, after deciding he would never learn, he took what he told himself would be his final shot. He made the shot quickly, eager to end his humiliation. He did it instinctively, just to get it over with. He simply pulled the arrow back, glanced at the target, and released the string. The arrow struck its mark.

And something had happened to him. For the briefest instant, the bow, the arrow, himself, and the target had all been one. Releasing the arrow had seemed the most natural thing he'd ever done. He'd felt a deep, almost mystical satisfaction as the arrow hissed on its way. In his mind, he'd already known that his aim was true.

And he'd begun to understand what the old man had meant.

From that day on, he'd truly become an archer—because he shot with his spirit, unselfconsciously, eager to recreate that timeless moment when the arrow perfectly left the bow and the world came together.

Fascinated, he read everything he could find about archery. The bow, along with the use of fire and the ability to speak, had been among the three most important developments in human history, someone had written—no doubt an archer. But there was logic to what he said. Because the bow perfected the hunt and made it possible for the race to survive.

And indeed the bow had existed for almost as long as human history—one hundred thousand years. Even more than the sword and the spear, the bow had been the basic weapon until the 1600s, when gunpowder and bullets began to replace it. The longbow, a tall straight shaft of wood that bent under pressure when the string was attached to it, had been the type that he had learned to shoot with—as old as the Norman victory over the English at the Battle of Hastings in 1066.

But there were other types, and he had made it his business—in later years, *literally* his business—to learn about them. In the late 1940s, a modern version of a bow type that the Assyrians had used as long ago as 1800 B.C. had begun to be popular at tournaments. It was called the recurve bow—because, when the bow was strung, its top and bottom limbs curved away from the archer.

It was different from the longbow in another way as well. It came in three pieces—a handle onto which the two limbs could be bolted securely. This three-part design made it possible for the bow to be disassembled and stored or carried in a compact space. But there was another, more useful logic to this three-part design. The handle, which didn't need to bend, could be made from a nonflexible material such as metal. The limbs, which did need to bend, could be made from a flexible substance such as wood, Fiberglas, or a combination of them. This construction resulted in a greater concentration of energy in the bow, and thus a faster, truer shot.

To him, the recurve design seemed the ultimate in archery. He perfected his skill with it, just as he had with the longbow. But after he returned from his ordeal in Nam, he discovered that the world had changed in more ways than he'd expected. As he'd said to Murdock back at the Wolf Den, "That's the thing about weapons. They always get more advanced." And the new development in archery was as big a leap from the recurve bow as the recurve bow had been from the longbow.

It was called a compound bow. It came in three pieces, as the recurve did—metal handle with two wood-Fiberglas adjoining limbs. But there the similarity with the recurve ended. For one thing, the end of each limb was slotted and curved toward the archer instead of away. For another, and crucial, the slotted end of each limb was equipped with an eccentric cam wheel. These wheels were interconnected with a cable which attached to the bow string.

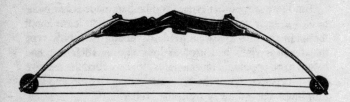

In effect, the archer faced what appeared to be three strings stretched taut before him, though he used only one to draw the arrow. He never had to bend the bow to attach the string. It and the cable were already secured to the wheels. If the archer disassembled the bow into handle and limbs, all he had to do to make the bow functional again was to snap each limb into its handle slot, turn each limb bolt (always being careful to balance the pressure, one turn at the top, one turn at the bottom, one turn at the top, one turn at the bottom, until the limbs were balanced), and as the limbs became secured, the cable and string would automatically tighten around the eccentric wheels.

And why the wheels? Because as the archer drew the bow, the wheels—like a system of pulleys—helped to ease his effort. But not all at once. At a standard thirty-inch draw, the archer's effort would remain the same until twenty-seven inches. Then the force he exerted, when he most needed it, would be reduced dramatically—by fifty percent. At a full thirty-inch draw, sixty pounds of effort would dwindle to thirty. The archer could hold his aim more easily.

And that wasn't all. When the archer let go of the string, the bow would release its energy in a more controlled fashion, adding thrust from thirty to sixty pounds instead of applying the sixty pounds all at once.

And why was that important? Because an arrow, receiving full thrust all at once (as in the longbow and the recurve bow), temporarily fought the assault. For a micro-instant, it stayed in place. It even buckled. And then shot forward. But energy had been wasted. The exertion of pressure was not efficient.

But not with the compound bow, which is why it was given that name. The wheels on the compound bow compounded the thrust as the arrow was propelled. Instead of hesitating for a micro-instant and even buckling, it accepted the thrust of the bow and shot ahead as perfectly fast and straight as was presently possible.

Murdock had joked about slingshots and spears and bows and arrows. But the fact was, the compound bow made an awesome weapon. In this case, it had been designed to require a hundred pounds of effort for the string to be pulled. Few archers could accomplish that, though Rambo could. He needed all the punch that the bow could deliver. The arrow would streak at two hundred and fifty feet per second. It could kill a man instantly. It could take down a Kodiak bear.

The bow he'd been given had special modifications. The Ram bow, he'd allowed himself to joke when he first tested it outside the Wolf Den. Like his knife, it was black (electrostatically painted, so the dark finish would not scrape off) to prevent a glint from it attracting an enemy's attention. Its handle was magnesium, as strong as aluminum alloy but with much less weight. Its limbs were carbonized Fiberglas with maple sandwiched at the core.

And because the handle was only twenty-one inches long, the limbs even shorter, eighteen inches, this compound bow when disassembled could fit into one of the twenty-two-inch quivers he'd strapped to each leg before he'd bailed out of the Peregrine jet.

As he watched Co's confused reaction, he used the straight-edged screwdriver on the guard of his knife to attach the bow's limbs to its handle. He screwed the top and bottom evenly, switching back and forth, and then it was assembled.

Even in the night, black against black, it looked magnificent.

And in the second quiver? His arrows. And they could be taken apart as well, their full thirty inches unscrewed at the middle and reduced by half, thus allowing them to be completely contained within the second quiver, along with other equipment that he needed for them.

As he reassembled them, concentrating on their considerable unique other features, he couldn't ignore Co's mystified blinking.

He finally found it necessary to speak, simplifying. "Better than a rifle. No sound."

"But . . ." Co stopped blinking and stared now. In shock. "That *all* you have?"

He turned abruptly, sensing movement down there. As if a time-lapse photograph had sped to normal, a tower guard showed himself in the box in the tree on the right, talking to another guard who paced under him. A third guard stepped from the hut in the middle of the compound, scratching his groin suggestively as the whore on the cycle sputtered up to him.

And stooping, Rambo crawled over the trip wire leading to the Claymore mine.

Alarmed, Co whispered behind him, "You not going in there?"

Rambo turned, puzzled.

"Where your camera?"

"Lost it."

"But my orders . . . I thought . . . You not supposed to go in. Supposed to take pictures only."

"Can't."

"Then watch. You tell. Spooks believe you."

Rambo shook his head. "I have to be sure."

"But what about . . . ?"

Rambo waited.

". . . orders?" Co asked.

Orders. Rambo's intensive training insisted.

And the basis of that training was that, no matter what, you did what you were told.

Without obedience and discipline, a mission couldn't be successful.

Trautman's voice barked through his consciousness. "Yes, the mind's the best weapon. Always rely on it. *But obedience is mandatory.* We don't need any hot-doggers in our outfit. No super surfers. No hot rodders. Gentlemen, when I tell you to shit, you do it. On the spot. And if you drop your drawers first, I'll give you ten miles of laps till you get the idea that I *didn't* tell you to drop your drawers. I told you to shit. We base our operations on precision. You're a piece of machinery. Granted, machinery who can think. But you're still machinery. And within the parameters of the assignment, with allowance for invention, you do what the hell you're told. Because a lot of other talented machines depend on you for their lives."

Rambo's heart shrank with the fear (the single fear he admitted) that he might be letting down his truly real father. Born from him out of Bragg and horrendous tests under fire.

But under the circumstances . . . ?

Would Trautman give him ten extra miles of laps if . . . ?

Would the person he loved most, the *only* person he loved, disapprove of what he meant to do?

The prisoners! his mind kept screaming. For me, six months here was an eternity.

And they've been here even longer.

"When I lost the camera . . ." he whispered to Co.

And now it was her turn to wait.

Sweat beaded on his forehead. ". . . orders stopped." His guts felt wrenched. "People began."

Determined—

—feeling that he'd done the unthinkable, that he'd invited his father's hate—

—he clutched his bow and quiver of arrows and slipped through the undergrowth.

— 8 —

Feeling Co behind him, he moved down the densely forested slope, checking for other booby traps.

Slow. Take it slow and careful.

On level ground again, he sank to his chest and crawled. At once, a scream from the camp made him pause, its echo fierce. His stomach tightened. Through a clump of ferns, Co next to him, he tensely scanned the camp. Sweat rolled past his eyes.

Had the scream come from a prisoner? He couldn't tell. A scream was the true international language, sounding the same no matter who made it, American and Vietnamese alike.

But the four guards he saw didn't seem to think it unusual. They were even amused. The guard in the tower to Rambo's right glanced down at the sentry pacing beneath him and chuckled. "He offered me some of that wine he made. I'm glad I didn't drink it," he said in Vietnamese.

"Me, too." The other laughed. "The last time, it gave me gas. Both ends."

They thought this was hilarious.

"And him. It gives him bad dreams. He probably thinks he's seeing those giant spiders again."

"We ought to find one and dump it on his bunk."

They doubled over, laughing.

From the barracks on the right, the scream was repeated,

even more strident, diminishing to a moan.

Rambo gestured to Co to stay where she was, and staring toward the tower on the left, he saw the shadow of a guard up there sitting tilted back, probably on a bamboo bench, with his boots on the waist-high wall of the box.

He shifted in that direction, squirming through ferns and bushes, reaching the corner where the barbed wire veered back toward the cliff. Moving parallel to that section of wire but well concealed in the undergrowth, he passed the guard tower. One thing in his favor was that the camp had been designed with the guard towers facing inward—to keep prisoners from escaping rather than to look for someone breaking in.

Where the shadow of a massive tree blocked the moonlight, he crept to the wire, drew his knife, and levered it between the post and the rusted wire, using the saw-edge on the back of the knife to slice the metal. He slipped through the opening, sank to his stomach again, and crawled to the next row of wire. But here, because the wire wasn't secured to posts but only unrolled and allowed to spring up in circular tangles, he was able to squeeze through one of the loops, careful not to get snagged on the barbs.

When he'd been held captive, the prisoners' barracks had been on the left. Clutching his bow, he shifted through the darkness toward it. But he knew that something was wrong even before he got there. The building looked dilapidated. Vines covered the walls. Shutters dangled. Several sections of bamboo had fallen away, leaving gaps.

And the building was deathly quiet. Even if prisoners were sleeping in there, he should have heard *something*. A snore. A cot squeaking. A murmur in response to a dream or, rather, a never-ending nightmare.

He reached a gap in the wall, stared in, and clenched his teeth. The building was filled with nothing but spider webs and vegetation that had grown up between the slats in the floor. An unseen animal skittered in the farthest darkest corner.

Co had been right. This building was in such bad shape

that the camp must have been abandoned for quite a while. The soldiers must have only recently come back.

But why?

And if there were prisoners, where were they being kept?

He crouched at the side of the barracks, waited for a guard to go by, gave him lots of time to leave the area, then crept toward the barracks in the middle of the camp. At the rear, hugging the wall, he slowly stood, showing only one eye as he peered above a window ledge.

The room was dark. Several guards slept on cots shielded by mosquito netting, their rifles stacked near the door against the opposite wall. One guard snored raucously, suddenly stopped, and slapped at something on his cheek. With a grunt, he turned onto his side and started snoring again.

Outside, Rambo lowered himself to a crouch and swung in surprise, hearing music from the next window. A scratchy phonograph record—a Vietnamese rock-and-roll band banging at out-of-tune guitars, singing a translated version of "Twist and Shout." A light came on, streaming from that window.

He didn't dare show himself to look in. Instead, he sank all the way to the ground and snaked toward the two-foot opening under the barracks, squirming through mud and spider webs. And maybe snakes themselves. The light from the room filtered down past the slats in the floor. He lay on his back and squinted up through a crack.

Though he couldn't see the whole room, he saw enough. Above him, a North Vietnamese soldier, a sergeant, had his back turned while he opened a tiny ancient refrigerator and took out a can of . . .

Coke, Rambo saw. Though the label had Chinese characters, the design of the logo on the can was unmistakable. Cold moisture beaded on it.

Something else was unmistakable. The face of the soldier. Rambo clutched his bow so hard his knuckles ached. Rage scalded his stomach, hate making him hold his breath. The tall thin sergeant—his face gaunt, his lips and nostrils perpetually sneering, his narrow eyes profoundly cruel—

was Tay, the soldier who'd most loved to torture him, who indeed had tried to flay him alive, who'd given him the scars, the reminders, on his chest and back.

Rambo knew he couldn't possibly be wrong. He'd seen that face, with its bad breath and its scummy teeth, too close to his own too often. He'd seen it leering grotesquely before him too many times in his sleep. On occasion, when Rambo's strength of will had not been great enough to maintain the mental discipline, the blessed escape, of Zen, he'd distracted himself—here, and in the town back in America, and in the quarry—with ways to get even with this man.

But after all this time, shouldn't Tay have been transferred? Shouldn't he have been stationed somewhere else?

When Rambo figured out the answer, it gave him satisfaction. Tay, you must have screwed up, huh? Whatever you did, it must have been so disgraceful that your punishment was to stay here in hell.

And if I get the chance, buddy, I'll add to it.

Tay rolled the cold can across his sweaty forehead, popped it open, and drank greedily. Foam ran from his lips and down the can, dripping toward the floor.

Between the cracks.

Past Rambo's eyes.

A woman spoke angrily, stepping into view. The whore from the village who'd arrived on the cycle. In Vietnamese, she said, "Hey, save some for me."

Tay tilted the can above his lips, stopped swallowing, burped, and tossed her the hollow-sounding can. "Here, take what's left."

He shoved her onto a cot, stalked toward her, unbuckling his belt, and snapped off the light.

The scratchy record kept blaring. Twist and shout.

— 9 —

The barracks on the right contained no prisoners either, only
other sleeping soldiers, and in one compartment, a solitary
man—the commander, Rambo assumed.

But if there aren't any prisoners, why the hell are all
these soldiers . . . ?

His attention focused on the cliff at the rear of the camp,
on the deeper blackness of a cave.

And he understood.

Cautious, reaching it, he found bamboo bars across the
entrance. And beyond, in the moldy wet recess . . .

He swallowed sickly. Anger flared in him.

Five Americans.

But, Jesus, they looked like . . .

Rotting zombies. Living corpses. Gaunt, covered with
scabs and running sores. The flesh on their chins and cheeks
had shrunk till their faces looked like skulls. By contrast,
their eyes seemed enlarged, bulging pathetically from bony
sockets. But their clothes didn't hang on them. Exactly the
reverse. Their ragged peasant clothes, too small, clung tight,
hitched grotesquely high on their arms and legs.

One of them, bathed in sweat, moaned, rolling on the
rock floor, wracked by malarial spasms. Another had wrapped
himself into a fetal position, his face between his knees.

Rats moved among them.

No, Rambo thought. I knew they'd look bad.

But I never guessed—

Even after his escape, after his six-week ordeal trudging

through the rain forest struggling to get below the DMZ, he'd never looked *that* bad.

His shock abruptly changed, becoming triumph. POWs. He could prove they existed. He'd found them.

Instinctively, he raised his knife to cut the ropes that held the bamboo bars in place. Hurry! he thought. Come on! I'll get you out of here!

But though their delirious eyes were angled in his direction, they didn't see him.

Or, worse, for all he knew, their blurred consciousness told them that he was just another guard, perhaps come to torture them again, and even that possibility they accepted passively.

He couldn't risk trying to get them out. One was sure to start babbling. Or another to moan. Or a third to stumble and fall, unable to raise himself.

That would get us all killed, Rambo thought.

Or put me back in here.

And that he could not endure.

But he had to do *something*.

Yes.

What I was told to do. Find out where the prisoners are being held. Get my ass back to the pickup site. And report to Murdock.

Delta Force will get these men out.

Because the POWs exist! I've seen them! I can prove it!

Prove it? he suddenly wondered, frowning. How? I don't have the camera.

Then I'll describe what I've seen.

And will they believe you? Trautman, of course.

But Murdock? The committee who ordered this mission?

They think my wrapper's loose to start with. No, they'll say my word—the word of a convict, of someone who shot up that town—isn't good enough.

Thanks, but no, thanks. Close, but no cigar.

But I have to do something. I have to bring some kind of proof.

And then he heard it.

A moan.

Beside him.

Close.

In the dark outside the cave.

— 10 —

He pivoted defensively, his knife raised. But what he saw made him lower it. Near a pigsty, a prisoner hung from a bamboo cross, his arms tied in a V above his head. The angle was deliberate, calculated. If his arms had been tied to the right and left in the form of a cross, the position of his muscles combined with the weight of his body would not have allowed him to breathe. A few hours after being hung up, he'd have suffocated.

But this other position, his arms up in a V, reduced the pressure on his chest.

He would suffer.

But not die easily.

The suspended man was ghostly white, a living skeleton. The leather that bound his wrists above him had abraded his skin, blood flowing down his arms. The cuts would leave scars. Rambo knew—because his own wrists bore the scars from being hung in this position.

Another reason to pay back Sergeant Tay.

The man wasn't moving. But as Rambo touched the broomstick bones of his neck, feeling for a pulse, the prisoner's eyes fluttered open.

Flickering. Focusing. His lips were cracked. A horrible bruise swelled around his left eye. "What . . . ?" His voice was raspy, guttural, faint.

Rambo clamped a hand across his mouth as he cut the lashings on the bamboo cross. The man fell into his arms. To grab him, Rambo had to take his hand from the prisoner's mouth.

"You . . . ?" The voice was barely audible, even close to Rambo's ear. "American?"

"Shh!" Rambo risked two further sounds. "Don't talk."

He hoisted the prisoner over his shoulder—it wasn't difficult; the man weighed almost nothing—and moved off in a crouching run.

"There are . . . others," the faint voice murmured, less than a whisper.

Don't worry, Rambo thought as he crept past the ruin of what used to be the prisoners' barracks. I give you my word. They'll be rescued.

Rambo's scrotum shrank as a searchlight came on, sweeping across the compound, heading his way. Caught in the open, Rambo had no other choice. His heart pounding, he set down the prisoner, hurriedly slipped an arrow onto his bow, and drew the string back.

The arrow was as sophisticated as his bow. Its shaft was made—not from wood, which would warp in the damp of this forest, and not from Fiberglas, which could shatter, but—from space age aluminum, strong yet not heavy, anodized black like the bow so there wouldn't be a dangerous reflection. It had a four-bladed, razor-sharp, saw-edged blade, one inch wide, two and a half inches long, anodized black like his bow and shafts. The serrations on the blades were designed to stop the broadhead from glancing off bone. Called a Copperhead Ripper, this head would imbed itself into almost anything. It had the penetrating capabilities of a copper-jacketed bullet.

He set the arrow against the soundless rubber rest on the compound bow's handle.

In Zen, the most powerful, disturbing, complicated figure is the archer. A bow that even the strongest man cannot pull back is easily worked by the frailest, most seemingly ineffectual monk. With the discipline of meditation, with the strength of mind over matter, and the solace of knowing that nothing is real—including the bow—the monk draws back the string, concentrating his intense imagination on the target that doesn't exist. He releases the arrow, and with a spine-chilling thrum, hiss, thunk, the shaft strikes home, always precise, always with the same religious meaning. Nothing—even violence—is real.

The guard in the box in the tree took the fiercely barbed arrow through his chest. The shaft stopped at the soft black nylon fletches (unlike feathers, they wouldn't wilt and lose their accuracy in this humidity), the impact so shocking that he never had the chance—even reflexively—to scream. He lurched back, disappearing.

The searchlight stopped, frozen on an insect on a fern.

Rambo frantically hoisted the prisoner once more and sneaked through the dark toward the barbed wire.

But the sentry, who had earlier passed the ruined barracks, paused as he noticed that the searchlight itself had paused. Rambo saw him squint up from the illuminated fern to glance suspiciously the other way, and then this.

In an eye blink, Rambo threw his knife—in this case toward the throat. The shock of the impact would not be sufficient to quell a scream unless...

The throat. Vocal cords severed, clutching his neck, eyes rolling upward, the guard toppled back.

Rambo hurried to retrieve his knife. Withdrawn, it dripped blood.

He shifted closer to the wire. Snick. The saw-teeth on his knife broke the unsecured inner row. He scrambled forward.

But a searchlight suddenly gleamed from the opposite guard tower, veering in his direction.

Jesus!

Oh, Jesus!

Dropping the prisoner, who coughed and groaned, Rambo nocked another arrow onto his bow, exerted the hundred pounds of effort necessary to pull back the string, and sent the deadly barbs hissing toward their target.

He knew he'd struck home when the searchlight tilted crazily toward the sky.

He also knew that the searchlight's position would warn the other soldiers. Five seconds—maybe—to get the fuck out of here.

— ‖ —

Co's heart pounded sickly against the pungent earth as she peered through ferns toward the compound. She'd been waiting, it seemed, for two hours, though a part of her knew that not more than fifteen minutes could have passed. The camp had remained lazily the same as it was at the start when the whore from the village had stepped inside the middle barracks. But somewhere within the compound, she was terribly aware, Rambo was searching. She tensed when she saw the searchlight on her left streak through the night and begin to scan the barracks. She held her breath when the searchlight stopped moving and instead glared straight down at the earth. She winced when she saw the searchlight on her left flick on abruptly, aim toward the opposite side of the camp, and inexplicably veer up toward the sky.

A shout of alarm broke the silence.

And a heavy boot stomped painfully down on her arm. She jerked, stifling a groan, and stared up, frightened.

At a puzzled but extremely angry Vietnamese soldier who aimed his AK-47 toward her face.

The guard's trigger arm moved as he tightened his grip to shoot.

And an eerie hissing sound ended with a dull ripping whump. An arrow seemed to materialize from his neck. He stood in place, the arrow pinning him to a tree. The rifle clattered onto the ground. He shuddered, blood spurting from an artery.

And Rambo was suddenly next to her, carrying a man slumped across his shoulder, his bow clutched rigidly.

He gestured sharply toward the ridge they'd used to get here. But the motion wasn't necessary. Co was already moving.

Behind, from the camp, a whistle shrieked. Then another. Soldiers yelled.

Her sphincter muscle contracted. Grabbing a tree root, she desperately scrambled up the slope.

But despite her fear and despite the dark, she noticed something. Even with the man he carried—blood roared behind her ears—Rambo kept ahead of her.

— 12 —

"Just remember, Colonel," Murdock said behind him. "You asked to go along. I advised you not to. It's your—excuse the expression—funeral."

Trautman didn't even bother turning. Angry, anxious, he

shoved the .45 pistol into the holster on his belt and continued out of the hangar. There wasn't much difference between the glow of the instruments he'd just left and the moonlight he faced.

To the left of the hangar, Ericson and Doyle were peeling the camouflage net off the Agusta 109 chopper. Ericson scrambled in, then Doyle. The powerful turbines began to warm up, whining with an ascending shriek that became a roar.

Reaching them, climbing in, Trautman said, "You cowboys waited long enough. It's minus *one* hour to extraction."

"Hey," Doyle said, chewing gum, but despite the gum, his breath suggested the resin of marijuana. "You gotta face reality. You know? Your boy's a helluva guy. I mean Flash Gordon. But he's probably splattered all over that forest. This joyride is just a favor. To you. You know?"

"Cool it, why don't you?" Ericson said and turned to Trautman. "My buddy's not exactly what you'd call diplomatic. What he's trying to say—we're probably just wasting fuel."

"And what we're really wasting is *time,*" Trautman said. "Get this damned thing off the ground, or I'll fly it myself."

"Wooh-ah," Doyle said. "Have patience, have patience."

Ericson, at the controls, lifted the chopper off, Trautman's stomach sinking as if an elevator had vaulted through the roof of a building.

"Good old Nam," Doyle said. "The gift that keeps on giving."

— 13 —

Rambo—crosstrained as a medic—checked the prisoner as bulging eyes in hollow sockets tracked back and forth from Co to himself.

They'd stopped when the shouts seemed safely behind them, catching their breath, orienting themselves.

"You guys are..."—the prisoner's voice was pathetically weak—"...real. Right?"

"Believe it," Rambo said, flexing the muscles in his back, relieving their ache, preparing to lift this man again.

"Sorry. I mean..." The prisoner fought to inhale. He licked his lips. "I talk to people all the time. My girl friend. My mom. My...dad."

"Just take it easy. Don't talk."

"Christ, how old must they be?" His logic shifted abruptly. "I know a lot of them aren't there. But this...is real? Isn't it? You're taking me home now?"

Home, Rambo thought. What's home?

"Yeah. Home."

"Thank God."

"Who *are* you?"

"Banks. Lieutenant. Air force." Banks sat frozen for a moment, blinking in disbelief, on the verge of tears. "Thank you. Christ. You're a miracle."

— 14 —

Breathing quickly, they stumbled through the rain forest, burst through underbrush, and lurched down the bank to the sampan.

Kinh seemed surprised to see them.

"What are you waiting for?" Rambo's voice was hoarse. "Crank that motor. Get this sucker moving."

"The money," Kinh demanded.

Co gave it to him.

"There. That better," Kinh said and whipped around to snarl orders at his men.

The engine sputtered into life. The sampan listed from the shore, straightened its balance, and headed—with the aid of the current—through the dark. Downriver.

As the crew, barely able to keep their balance because they were even more drunk, watched puzzled, Banks leaned his head against a crate and spoke in English.

"Gotta tell you. Just luck."

"What?" Rambo asked.

"You guys came when you did. They..." Banks groaned. "See, they move us around a lot. To build roads and harvest crops. Only been there a week."

"Where?"

The motor kept chugging, the sampan increasing speed through moonlight reflecting off the shadows of the rain forest and the river.

"The camp," Banks said. "What's the matter?"

"Only a week?"

"Yeah. Jesus, I hate that place."

Co interrupted. "When last time you in camp there?"

Banks frowned, his shrunken skin making his expression more emphatic. "Maybe a year. Hey," he realized. "What year *is* it?"

Rambo told him.

"No . . . That can't be right . . . Not that long. No."

"Camp all that time empty?" Co asked.

Banks nodded.

Co glanced disturbed at Rambo.

"Yeah, I know what you're thinking," Rambo said.

"What? Something wrong?" Banks asked and wheezed.

"Nothing you need to worry about."

Sure.

Not you. Just us, Rambo thought.

"Gotta smoke?"

"Don't use it," Rambo said. To distract himself, he asked, "So why were you on the cross?"

"Well, I caught this cobra, see . . ."

"Snake?" Co asked, alarmed.

"Yeah. Snake." Banks coughed. "It's not hard once you get the hang of it. In the wrist." He seemed delirious. "All in the wrist . . . Anyway, I did what I always do. When I get one."

Rambo frowned. "What's that?"

Banks giggled. "Put it in the guards' barracks."

Rambo stared.

"Man . . ."—Banks giggled harder, wheezing—". . . do they get pissed. They beat the livin' crap out of me. But . . ."

Rambo glanced nervously toward the dark shore.

". . . it's kind of a tradition. Know what I mean? You oughta see 'em run around."

"You've got," Rambo said, "what the brass calls a bad attitude."

"Yeah, ain't it the truth?" Banks chortled. "Christ, I can't believe . . ." He gazed with reverence up at Co. "Hey, thanks, lady. You know, don't take this wrong, you're kinda cute. I haven't seen a woman since . . ."

Co gingerly touched his shrunken battered cheek. "Don't talk, please. Rest."

"But . . . what are you doin' Saturday?"

Rambo noticed how she swallowed thickly. She glanced his way. A tremor made her pajamas tremble.

"I bring you food, Banks." She stood, agitated. "Good food." She pursed her lips, feigning anger. "But you eat slowly." Jerked a finger insistently. "Not get sick."

Rambo almost grinned with admiration for her.

But the growing roar of a powerful engine burst his impulse. He grabbed for his pistol. His heart cramped, thumping, speeding despite the pressure. A searchlight gleamed.

– 5 –

THE SLIME PIT

— I —

Whatever was out there, it wasn't an enemy patrol boat. That would have been bad enough. But this thing . . . The motor's rumble made it sound huge. The shadow behind its powerful searchlight seemed to stretch back forever. Hearing the pirate crew murmur, Rambo grabbed his bow, raised Banks to his shoulder, and darted toward the entrance to the cabin. The searchlight, streaking across the water, had not yet found the sampan. If he got inside before it did, there was still a chance that he and Banks could hide, that Kinh could offer bribes the same as before.

But as he ducked past the canvas sheet at the cabin's entrance, he glanced back, and now the thing out there was rumbling so close that he saw what it was. No, not a patrol boat. Not at all. He caught just a quick glimpse of it, but that was enough. Good Christ, the thing was a U.S. Navy gunboat, massive, the barrels of cannons and machine guns silhouetted in the moonlight. But the U.S. Navy didn't own it any longer. The Communists had salvaged it from the war. And they knew how to handle it.

Inside the fetid dark of the cabin, he stopped beside Co, who'd come in here to get food for Banks, and whose eyes now were wide with alarm as she tried to see past the curtain toward the powerful rumbling engine.

"What is . . . ?" Co started to say.

And the darkness added to the confusion. Rambo felt a rifle against his back. A hand yanked his .45 from its holster. Someone threw Co against a crate as Banks was flung to the cluttered floor, where he gasped and lay still.

"You wanted to know what's happening?" Rambo told Co, his voice hoarse with rage. "Kinh sold us out."

Indeed, outside on the deck, Kinh was shouting in Vietnamese to the gunboat. "Over here! Over here!" He barked to one of his men, "Take the helm!"

And stepped inside the cabin. As the searchlight settled gleaming upon the sampan, Rambo saw that for once Kinh wasn't toothlessly grinning. "American pig!"

Kinh spat in Rambo's face. The greasy saliva smelled foul. Enraged, Rambo almost lunged to smash the son-of-a-bitch's larnyx, but another weapon was abruptly rammed against him from behind, this time the larger bore of a shotgun twisting against the back of his head.

"What made you wait so long?"

"They found us. I make a deal with them. Better deal than *you* make."

"What?"

"Better than money. My life. American pig!" he yelled louder, obviously hoping the soldiers would hear him. "Business is business." He shrugged and slapped Rambo viciously across the face.

Kinh's mistake. Not because it made Rambo angrier. But because it allowed him to twist with the force of the blow, to pretend that he'd lost his balance, which of course he hadn't. Pivoting with the skill of a dancer, he nudged the rifle and shotgun away from him, drove an elbow back, shattering one pirate's rib cage, and continued swinging around, now with his knife out, and it was sharp enough, it cut off the second pirate's head. While blood sprayed as if from a broken hydrant, the head thumped onto the hollow floor, the shotgun clattering, and Rambo was already grabbing for it. Sensing Co grab for the rifle, Rambo glared at Kinh racing out the door. Pulled the shotgun's trigger. And at close range, the blast amplified by the confines of the cabin, blew Kinh in half. In a mist of blood, Kinh's upper torso flipped back into the cabin. The bottom seemed to take two steps forward and toppled toward the rail.

Rambo leaped over the pieces and burst through the doorway onto the deck. The shotgun had a pump action. He chambered a shell, blasted the face off a pirate. Pumped and blew another off the deck into the water. Pumped and blasted the searchlight streaking closer.

It shattered, glass imploding. Darkness returned. He heard frantic shouts from the gunboat, and something else, close behind him, the stuttering volley from an AK-47. Spinning in a crouch to return the pirate's fire, he saw splinters erupting from the bamboo wall of the cabin, bullets hitting a pirate who had grabbed an axe and started to lunge this way, the pirate flipping over the railing into the water. Co suddenly appeared at the cabin's entrance, her AK-47 aimed for another burst.

An explosion shattered the front of the sampan, wood flying, making Rambo list. The gunboat had opened fire. His ears rang from the deafening blast.

"Get Banks!" Rambo shouted to Co. "Get him over the side!"

He rushed inside the cabin, and as Co dragged Banks out onto the deck, he jerked open the greasy wooden locker, grabbing the rocket launcher. He slipped a cylinder into the tube and armed it.

Hearing more gunfire, he raced out to where Co was shooting at the gunboat.

"Take him and jump!" Rambo shouted.

He ducked toward the back of the sampan just as a second explosion ruptured what was left of the front. Water sprayed over him. The sampan was sinking.

Co slung her rifle over her shoulder, lifted Banks, and went over the side, with a splash enveloped by the muddy water.

And Rambo raised the rocket launcher to his shoulder. Even in the dark, the massive gunboat now rumbled so close that he couldn't miss. He pulled the launcher's trigger, felt the weapon jerk on his shoulder, and saw the reflection of a belching flame behind him, as ahead of him the gunboat's superstructure erupted with a brilliant roar. Night became day, pieces of metal and bodies streaking toward the sky. Quick secondary explosions followed—munitions, he assumed—and then with a *whump!* the fuel tank blazed.

But the fucker wasn't sinking. Like a fiery Flying Dutchman ghost ship, it just kept coming, and coming, and . . .

Rambo dropped the rocket launcher, grabbed his bow and quiver from inside the cabin, and sprinted toward the stern as . . .

The gunboat struck the wreckage at the front, jolting the sampan, the impact adding to Rambo's thrust as he dove from the stern. His face struck the muddy water, his body plunging in and down and forward, and even underwater he heard yet another roar. When he surfaced, his face covered with grit and scum from the river, he smelled gasoline and almost turned to study the blazing gunboat and sampan when his eyes widened at the sight of soldiers on the shore. Illuminated by the flames, they gaped, appalled. Some pointed. Others rushed into the water as if in hopes of finding survivors.

And Rambo, his head barely showing, nervously allowed the current to take him, drifting tensely, staring along the shore for a sign of . . .

Co. Farther down, he saw where she crouched behind soggy driftwood, hiding at the mouth of a stream. Banks lay next to her, his legs showing through a gap in some bushes. Co's chest heaved, out of breath, frightened, exhausted.

Silently, feeling the weight of his wet clothes and boots dragging him down, he swam with a powerful breaststroke, touched squishy bottom, and crept from the river to the shelter of the driftwood at the mouth of the stream.

Even here, the whoosh of the burning gunboat and sampan was so enormous that they could risk a few hurried whispers.

"Are you all right?" he asked Co.

She sagged, her energy depleted, in shock.

"I asked..."

"Very bad."

"What's...?"

"I kill. Lose many merits in next life. Very bad."

"No, it depends on who you kill. That wasn't a 'who.' That was an 'it.' An animal."

Sprawled in the bushes, Banks murmured, "What the hell...?"

"Fourth of July."

He coughed weakly. "Yeah, I think I remember that. Trick or treat."

"We have to move," Rambo said, lifting him.

"Or is that when you wear the white beard and red suit?"

Carrying Banks over one shoulder, clutching the quiver and bow in his other hand, Rambo struggled, Co beside him, away from the shimmering blaze, working toward the dark of the forest.

The pickup site, he was thinking, muscles sore, legs stiff, lungs desperate for air. Have to reach the pickup site.

Behind him, he heard a distant shout. Then another one. Not so far this time.

He rushed.

— 2 —

His lips pursed, tense, Trautman sat behind Ericson, watching him work the Agusta 109 chopper's controls. It whump-whump-roared at treetop level across a black forested valley, rising and dropping with the terrain. The cockpit panel was dark.

"Can't you go any faster?" Trautman asked.

"Hey, I've got this baby cranked to a hundred and fifty already."

Ahead, a faint illumination silhouetted the mountainous horizon.

"Besides, you said it yourself," Ericson added. "We've got a schedule to keep. We get there any sooner than we're supposed to—assuming your boy's alive and made it to the extraction site—we won't be doing him any favors. Us neither. Every Cong in the neighborhood'll wonder what the hell and check us out."

Ericson almost had to shout to be heard in the roar of air past the open bay behind them.

Trautman turned in that direction. Doyle, secured by a safety line, sat with his legs dangling out the bay, his pant legs flapping from the windstream. Beyond, below, the forest was a close dim blur. Doyle's hair fluttering, he leaned toward the mounted M-60 beside him and racked the bolt, arming it. He seemed to sense that his gesture had attracted attention and glanced toward the front, toward Trautman surveying him.

"Just entered Injun country." Doyle grinned.

The horizon slowly brightened.

— 3 —

As the sun rose higher, Rambo scrambled up an incline, his shoulder in pain from carrying Banks, his body drenched with sweat.

Co parted bushes, scanning the landscape ahead of them. Nodding, she hurried forward.

The vista was stunning. They'd reached an escarpment. To the right, a cliff dropped a hundred feet to the river. On the opposite side of the river, a stream cascaded over another cliff, glinting in the sun as it tumbled misting into a picturesque lagoon.

Directly ahead, though, was a clearing, and that was more beautiful than the waterfall.

Because the clearing was the pickup zone.

Finding cover behind vine-covered rocks, Rambo eased Banks onto the ground and straightened, flexing his shoulder, trying to ease the terrible muscle cramps. He breathed deeply several times.

But all the while, his gaze was concentrated back in the direction from which they'd come—down the steep slope, toward the valley...

And the dim specks of soldiers charging through undergrowth, their shouts reverberating through the forest.

Well, he thought. He had to give somebody credit. Whoever was guiding them, maybe a villager, maybe a soldier, was a damned fine tracker. Fifteen minutes, no longer, and they'd be up here.

He slowly turned in a circle, staring at every sector of the horizon.

But where the hell was the chopper?

He studied his bow and the quiver of arrows, then shifted his gaze toward Co's AK-47. "I won't be needing this now. Tell you what. Trade you."

"Helicopter come soon."

"Sure." He shrugged. "I bet. But just in case."

She handed over the rifle.

He exchanged with her. "There's a pack of C-4 explosive in the quiver. Don't worry, though. It can't explode without a detonator."

"I know. Spooks train me how to use it."

"Good."

In the valley, the shouts were a little louder, closer.

"Well," Rambo said. "You better take off."

On the ground, Banks murmured, "What? You mean you ain't coming out with us?"

"My orders are stay in-country. But maybe..."

Rambo raised his eyebrows in question.

"...it better I wait till end. Help, maybe."

Rambo glanced toward the frantic specks of the soldiers charging through the undergrowth in the valley. He didn't hear even the faintest faraway roar of a chopper. "End? This *is* the end."

"But I *want* to stay." She gestured impatiently. "Forget orders. Now I have chance. You take me back?"

He didn't understand. "Back? Where?"

"America. You can do this if you want. Take me back. As wife."

To Rambo, the word was shocking. He couldn't comprehend the enormity. It threatened him. It...

"You not understand. Not live with me. Just help me get away there. Huntington Beach. See my brother." Her voice shook. "More important, see my son. You divorce. You say I no good wife. But I now citizen. I stay."

Even to him, his excuse sounded weak. "But I came for POWs. I mean...How would it look if I came back with a wife?"

"Look?" She straightened proudly. "Look like you one hell of a man."

He shook his head, even more threatened.

"What the matter? Not allow yourself to feel? Maybe dead inside already? We not die soon enough?" She gestured toward a purple moth-orchid in a cluster of them at a swampy edge of the forest. "You see. My code name—Orchid. A flower like that need good soil to grow. Many time under earth is bones of animal ... or person. Killed in forest. Make soil rich. Grows most beautiful flower. You call orchid. Many deaths in forest. Vietnamese. V.C. American. Many beautiful flowers. But I hope stay alive. Not beautiful but hope ... stay alive. Not want to die."

Rambo jerked his head toward the shouts from the valley.

"Maybe sooner than you think," he said.

Like a heartbroken child, she peered at the ground. "Just thought I'd ask."

And Rambo felt what for him a day ago would have seemed an impossible emotion. His own heart felt broken.

She surprised him, leaning close, kissing him on the cheek.

And even more surprising, he allowed her. The closest he'd been to a woman in the last fourteen years. The feel of her lips on his cheek was like an electrical jolt. Her subtle breath caused goose bumps on his skin.

Clutching the bow and the quiver of arrows, she started across the sunlit clearing toward the shadowy continuation of the forest. Her tiny black-pajamaed figure got smaller.

"Come on, man," Banks said. "What the fuck's the matter with you? Let's take her with us."

Rambo felt paralyzed. Defensive instincts fought with...

"All right," he said abruptly. "Stay. We marry. I divorce. You live in Huntington Beach."

She turned. She'd been weeping. But now, through her tears, she beamed. "You . . . hell of a good man."

"But you stay out of sight till the chopper arrives." *If*, he thought. *If* it arrives. He still didn't hear even a faint echoing murmur of its approach.

She nodded, seeming to understand. If the soldiers arrived before the chopper did, he was giving her a chance to save her life.

"Rambo, you not ex-pend-able."

"We'll soon find out."

And then he heard it, dim, far away, and there wasn't another sound—heart swelling—like it in the world. The rescue chopper.

His excitement burst when he heard strained breathing behind him, turned, and saw the first soldier charge over the top of the slope.

— 4 —

Trautman stared anxiously past Ericson toward the cliff beyond the canopy. "Come on!"

"Three minutes to pickup," Ericson said. He worked the controls, but instead of veering up the cliff to skirt its top as Trautman expected, Ericson streaked directly ahead toward a gorge.

"What the—?"

"Quicker this way. Didn't you say you wanted speed?"

At once they were in it, the cliffs on either side rebounding the chopper's roar, amplifying. The gorge was like a wind tunnel, bouncing, buffeting the chopper. Trautman braced himself. "The quicker, the better."

The chopper lurched.

In back, his legs still dangling from the open bay, Doyle whooped. "Here comes the cavalry!"

— 5 —

Aiming the AK-47, Rambo shot yet another soldier charging over the slope. He shouted to Co, "Get back!" The soldiers would have figured this out by now. Instead of coming up the slope, they'd circle around, take cover in the forest and . . .

Dragging Banks through the bushes around the clearing, searching for a semicircle of rocks that would give him better protection, he shouted again to Co, "Get back! The forest on the other side! Before the soldiers surround us!"

"But I want to go with you!"

"The soldiers will be here before the chopper is! Dammit, go! The deal's off! Get the hell out of here!"

Crouching behind low rocks, facing bushes that rimmed the slope, he saw frantic movement to his right, farther over. The soldiers. They'd scrambled up a different part of the slope. Darting through undergrowth now, they gained the strategic seclusion of the forest.

That's it, Rambo thought. It's almost over. He heard the increasing sound of the chopper. But too far away yet. He couldn't see it. And his rifle was just about empty.

If I didn't have Banks, I could get away, he thought.

But that was the problem. He did have Banks.

And he wasn't about to leave him.

He stared toward the clearing, toward where Co had been standing.

And that was one good thing at least.

She'd done what he'd said. She was gone.

— 6 —

The chopper rushed from the gorge. As the amplified deafening roar diminished to a merely unbearable noise, Trautman stared at the narrow valley below him, the treetops incredibly close, then saw another cliff looming ahead, and this time Ericson did veer up to skirt the wooded top.

"It should be . . . Yeah, ahead of us." Ericson pointed. "There."

Heart pounding, Trautman squinted. In the distance, past a stream cascading over a bluff, the bottom of which he couldn't see from this approach, he studied a clearing on an escarpment. A cliff flanked it on this side. A brush-covered slope was on the left. Beyond and to the right . . . rain forest.

A puff of dust rose from the clearing.

Another.

And yet another, this one among the bushes.

Ericson straightened. "What the hell's that?"

The clearing enlarged as the chopper streaked closer.

"It looks like . . ." Trautman frowned.

He saw the next puff of dust—it lifted rocks and tore apart bushes.

". . . a goddamned firefight."

Among the bushes, he saw a speck move, the minuscule figure of a man who lifted another man across his shoulder and waved a stick—a rifle?—in this direction.

A puff of dust threw the figure off his feet.

"Those are mortar explosions!" Trautman yelled. "He's under attack! Good Christ, it's Rambo! He made it!"

"Well, why don't we even the odds!" Doyle shouted, scrambling to his feet. With a grin, he aimed the M-60. "Just a little closer, baby!"

The pickup site became more large and clear with every second. Trautman saw Rambo aiming his rifle toward the forest, jerking with the weapon's recoil. Made soundless by the chopper's roar, the firefight looked eerie. He picked up the other figure, lurching through bushes toward the clearing.

"But who's he got with him?" Ericson asked. "There's not supposed to be . . . Holy shit, you don't guess . . ."

"That's . . . An American! Christ! Relay to command! He's found one! He's brought back one of ours!"

— 7 —

Murdock glanced again at his watch as he paced in front of the radio console in the hangar. Why in God's name were they taking so long? The chopper should have . . .

"Sir?" a technician said behind him.

Expectant, Murdock spun.

The technician tried to sound impersonal, though he was obviously excited. "I have an AWACs relay. Dragonfly reports they've sighted Rambo. He has what appears to be . . ."

"Well?" he blurted. "Go on."

"An American POW with him."

"What?" Murdock lunged toward the console.

"That's right, sir." The technician grinned broadly. "They've got one of ours."

Murdock's face went blank with shock. ". . . of ours?" In a rage, he swung toward the other technicians. "This station is now on Condition Bravo! Harrison! Meyers! Goodell! All of you! Out! Now!"

The technicians stared puzzled at him.

"Out, I said! Move your asses! Now!"

Half angry, half totally confused, they set down their headsets, gravitating toward each other, drifting toward the hangar's exit, glancing back.

"No, not you!" Murdock told the technician who'd spoken to him. "Go to your COMINT priority frequency! Give me that mike! Dragonfly!" he shouted into it. "This is Pack Leader at Wolf Den! This is an Alpha-Kilo-Victor command priority!"

Static crackled in the headset. Ericson's voice broke through it. "Roger, Pack Leader. Go ahead."

"I want you to abort the operation at once! Repeat! Abort at once! Return to Den!"

— 8 —

In the chopper rushing toward the pickup site, seeing Rambo fire another burst from his rifle at soldiers breaking from the forest, Ericson blinked, puzzled at the orders he'd just received. He adjusted his headset. "Say again, Pack Leader. Repeat."

"Abort! For fuck's sake, abort!" Murdock's static-riddled voice insisted.

That certainly sounded affirmative enough.

"Roger," Ericson said and turned to Trautman. "I've just been ordered not to pick them up."

"Not . . . ? He must be crazy!" Trautman said, his face leaning rigidly, savagely, close. "Confirm it!"

"That isn't necessary. Believe me, the orders are clear."

"My ass!"

Ericson felt his headset yanked off. His ears stung.

"Murdock!" Trautman yelled into the mouthpiece. "What the Christ is the matter with you? We have them in sight! We can get them, Murdock! We can *get* them! Do you read me!"

Ericson shrugged. "Man, go with the flow. I don't think he wants to listen. Hang on. We're turning around."

"You bastard, stay on your heading!"

"Sorry. Can't do that. Orders is orders."

"And *this*, believe it, is an order!" Trautman said.

"Man, relax, why don't you? We're not in the military. We're independent contractors. We take our orders from whoever pays. And right now, the boss says turn around."

"Mercenaries." Trautman puckered his mouth as if to spit. "There are *men* down there! *Our* men!"

"No, *your* men," Ericson said. He wasn't worried when Trautman grabbed for the .45 in a holster on his belt.

Because Doyle stood right behind him with an M-16 against Trautman's head.

"Hey, do what my friend here says, huh?" Doyle said. "Just relax and go with the flow. You keep getting all upset, you'll end up with an ulcer."

And with *that* taken care of, Ericson pivoted the chopper—so close to the pickup site that the wind from the rotors bent bushes—back toward a cool can of Bud.

— 9 —

Rambo stared in disbelief. As he carried Banks across his shoulder, running across the clearing—

—mortar explosions stunned him to the right and left—

—the Agusta 109 suddenly halted in its descent—

—he saw the pilot, Ericson, quite clearly shrug and wave—

—pivoted, and with a chugging roar, it streaked away.

"What the . . . ? Where's he . . . ?" Banks groaned on Rambo's shoulder. "Why—?"

"They sold us out."

"Oh, Jesus! The bastards left us?"

"We're on our own."

As Rambo dropped Banks, spinning with the AK-47, getting off two frustrating shots before the rifle no longer responded, out of ammunition, he silently cursed.

Yeah, we were sold out, all right.

The gunfire from the forest gradually diminished, a crack now and then, but nothing serious. The soldiers creeping angrily from their cover toward him, Rambo dropped the weapon and glanced a bleak last time toward the sky.

Toward the Agusta 109 sprinting its tail back to base. It diminished, becoming a dot.

But the soldiers came ever closer, rifles raised, furious.

And the angriest of all, the most outraged when he recognized the face of the man who had caused him so much trouble, recognized the face of the prisoner who years ago had escaped but only after his chest and back bore the scars of his knife, was Sergeant Tay.

And before the butt of an AK-47 viciously struck Rambo's forehead, knocking him flat on the ground, his skull in agony, he thought—his face was so consumed with rage that it must have seemed blank—

—If I live . . . and it's the reason I'll force myself, I'll *make* myself, to live . . . some son-of-a-bitch is going to pay for this.

— 10 —

From the forest on the far side of the clearing, hidden but close enough to see the sweat on the brows of the angry soldiers, Co clutched the bow and the quiver, her knuckles aching as she saw her man surrounded.

He managed to grope to his knees when a sergeant kicked him in the . . . she strained to find the English word . . . privates, crotch . . .

. . . balls.

Her heart ached as they kicked his back. His chest. His legs. She could feel the blows. She almost groaned in sympathy, but she kept her discipline as she knew her man would have kept his discipline.

Yes. Her man. She felt a bond between them—and understood why, at the end, he'd told her to leave. Not because he didn't want to take her to America. Oh, most surely, he would have.

But because, with the soldiers attacking and the helicopter so far away, though coming closer, he hadn't wanted to risk her life.

He'd meant to save her.

And now as the soldiers dragged her man away, along with the sobbing prisoner called Banks, she made a promise to herself.

More than a promise. A vow.

She raised a hand to the good-luck medallion on her neck.

Rambo, her man, had wanted to save her life.
And she, by Buddha, would save her man.

— II —

As polite as an order can be, Murdock slammed a glass of
Scotch down on the desk in his cubicle. "Sorry, no ice, but
have a drink."

"What are you doing?" Trautman shouted. "Do you know
what the hell you've done?"

"Know? Of course. But have you got five hours—ten?—
while I tell you about former administrations, and Secretaries of State, and Secretaries of this and that, and committees, and committees to fund committees, and diplomatic
relations, and . . . ?"

Trautman's cheeks rippled. "Take your time. As long as
Rambo's out there being crucified."

"Colonel, we're both adults. We both know the situation.
This is a war. Granted, a cold war. Subtle. But it's still a
war. And it's intense. And in war, well, people get sacrificed."

"Not *my* people."

"Sometimes. Hey, don't tell me you've forgotten Khe
Sanh. A piece of worthless real estate. But you . . ."

"Not *me*."

"Somebody! . . . allowed a lot of good men to get killed
in a stupid siege on a heap of mud that nobody really wanted.
A so-called strategic hill that in fact was worthless compared
to the cover of the forest around it. Didn't whoever planned

that operation remember the lesson Ho Chi Minh taught the French at Dien Bien Phu? Sacrifices? The military's had its share of making sacrifices. So don't kid a kidder, Colonel. And don't act so innocent about this mission. You're more intelligent than that. Surely you had your suspicions, and if you suspected but didn't object till it was over, that makes you an accessory, don't you think?"

Trautman threw the Scotch glass against the wall. It shattered—but to his credit, Murdock didn't flinch—whiskey fumes filling the narrow room.

"Don't ever count me with scum like you! The mission was a lie, wasn't it? Just like the whole damned war! A lie!"

"That's ancient history. Something the politicians decided."

Staring at Murdock's impassive face, Trautman tried to calm himself. "All right." He inhaled deeply. "So why did you pull the plug?"

"Me? Hey, no, not me. I've got my orders, too. I've got a mortgage, Colonel. A wife and kids. You think I like hurting people? I'm just doing a job. If I knew what's right and wrong, I'd be a goddamned priest, right? Maybe a rabbi and Billy Graham for added measure. I'm more practical. I follow directives from so-called wiser men. And women, too. I don't want to be a chauvinist. I do what I'm told, and that's what I expect from my subordinates. And if your boy—your nutso, as far as I'm concerned—had done what *he* was told, if he'd taken photographs and got his rear end out of there, we'd have picked him up. There wouldn't have been a problem."

"I want an explanation, dammit!"

Murdock stared.

Exhaled.

And sat.

"It was clean," he said. "Very. If Rambo said he couldn't find them, cool. And believe me, he wasn't supposed to. That camp was empty as far as we knew, and as a bonus, it was the camp he'd escaped from. It carried a lot of symbolic value—brave man risks his life to go to hell and back—a second time. If he got himself caught, why, he's a private citizen, a whacko, acting on his own. And if he somehow got lucky and did find proof, well, the proof would have been lost somewhere between Thailand and Washington. Airtight. Lean and clean. No POWs. The Congress buys it. The Legion of Families buys it. Maybe even the vets buy it. Except . . . Who could have figured that the camp was due to be reoccupied? And your boy had to be a hero. He wasn't satisfied with taking pictures. No, he had to bring back a souvenir. Can't stop being a hero. So I had to cancel. No choice."

"Terminate with extreme prejudice."

"That's a crock! The agency never said that! Never! Do you have any idea what would have happened if he brought that guy back? We're talking ransom here. In '72, when the war was winding down, we were supposed to pay four and a half billion dollars to North Vietnam to get those Americans back. That's billion. With a B, Colonel. For a few guys who've had their brains in a blender for a third of their lives. A pain in the ass to everybody. No way. There's just no way."

"So the ransom wasn't paid, and the same lies just keep on, and there never was a Phase Two rescue team."

"What the hell would you suggest we do if some burned-out POW shows up on the six o'clock news? Fight the war all over again? Have an armed invasion? Bomb Hanoi? Do you honestly think that anybody is going to get up on the floor of the United States Senate and ask four and a half billion dollars for a couple of forgotten ghosts? Have you read about the national deficit lately?"

"Ghosts?" Trautman's spine went rigid. "Were you ever in combat, Murdock? And don't give me that crap about the unit you claim you commanded in '66. You never got closer to the war than the six o'clock news. But *they* were in combat. And some of their buddies died in combat. But by comparison, *these* men weren't that lucky. They might wish every day with all their souls that they could die, but they're not ghosts yet, you bastard, and four and a half billion dollars or not, somebody *has* to bring them back."

Murdock shook his head. "It just isn't going to happen."

"God help you."

"This conversation's pointless." Murdock swallowed his own glass of Scotch. "I should have known it's useless to try to explain to, well, let's say, outsiders. You've got to give me credit, though. I tried. So I'm going to forget this conversation ever took place. I suggest you do the same. Don't bring this subject up again. You'd make a mistake."

"No, you're the one making a mistake."

"Yeah? What mistake?"

"I said God help you. I know him better than you do."

"Him?"

"You didn't figure on him. You should have. Rambo."

— 12 —

Groggy from repeated blows to his face, his vision blurred by pain, Rambo dangled from a bamboo cross, his arms tied above him, as Sergeant Tay's raging features loomed before him. For a moment, Tay seemed a rabid ferret in a nightmare. Then a shadow passed in front of the ferret, and Rambo's vision cleared sufficiently for him to see a knife, to recognize Tay's face, and his swirling mind convinced him that he'd never escaped from here, that he hadn't gone back to America, that the cop and the town hadn't been real or the prison, and he hadn't come back to Nam, he hadn't been recaptured. All of it had been an illusion, a hoax produced by delirium as Sergeant Tay persisted in trying to flay him but keep him alive.

But the knife kept getting closer, and Rambo's vision cleared even more, enough to identify the knife. Not Tay's but his own, its black blade distinctive, its saw-teeth on the back, its screwdrivers on the guard. And was that, too, part of the illusion? How could the knife be his if he'd never escaped and come back and been recaptured?

"Such a beautiful knife." Tay spoke in Vietnamese. "How kind of you to have brought me this present. How thoughtful. You must have missed me very much to have gone through so much trouble coming back here to give it to me."

Rambo's mind stopped swirling, everything clear now. Terribly so. The chopper veering away. The soldiers surrounding him. Tay striking him with a rifle butt.

"Where's Banks?"

Tay slapped his face. "Banks? You mean our prisoner who left without asking permission. He missed his friends so much that we finally gave in to his pleading and put him back with them."

"In the cave?" Dangling, his arms in agony, Rambo squinted past the buildings toward the cliff in back.

"Temporarily. He'll join us later. In the meantime we've arranged an entertainment. Indeed, an instructive example of what happens to prisoners who try to escape. I haven't forgotten, by the way. I still remember chasing you through the forest. Three days. But even as weak and sick as you were, you got away. My commander was furious. The other soldiers made jokes about me. I lost much face. Sometimes I think that's why I was never transferred out of . . ."—he scowled toward the rain forest, his mouth working as if to select a word bad enough to describe his surroundings— ". . . this."

A voice spoke from the side. Rambo turned as Tay did.

A Vietnamese captain approached from a building, his uniform immaculate, his bearing military-stiff, the only soldier in the camp who seemed determined to maintain his dignity. "Get on with it, Sergeant."

"I was just explaining the procedure, sir."

The officer stopped rigidly before Rambo. "My name is Captain Vinh. And your name . . . ?"

Rambo didn't answer.

"You will tell me soon enough. I've already contacted my superiors about your arrival. They want information. You obviously didn't come here on your own. A helicopter failed to pick you up. It had no markings. Who was in the helicopter? Who ordered you to come here?"

Rambo didn't speak.

"You will tell me. Soon."

Vinh gestured to Tay and stepped back as if he didn't want to sully his uniform. He wiped his hands.

Tay nodded, turned to Rambo, and held up the knife. "Perhaps you expect . . . ? The scars on your back and chest . . . ? Not this time. We've made an improvement in the camp. I think you should see it."

Bewildered, Rambo felt the bamboo crucifix being lifted by soldiers shoving down on a pole attached to it across a fulcrum. His feet dangled higher off the ground. He was swung to the left, the movement adding more strain to his arms.

And the bamboo crucifix stopped.

Hanging, peering down past his chest as it heaved straining for air, Rambo saw . . .

A pit.

It was eight feet wide. It went ten feet down. With the burning sun at its zenith above him, he saw the floor of the pit quite clearly.

No shadows. Nothing to distort what he saw, to play tricks with his vision.

And yet . . .

He was sure that his eyes indeed were playing tricks.

Because the floor of the pit was moving.

Snakes, he thought at first. But he knew, he could plainly see, that snakes weren't causing the movement.

A ripple.

A rise and fall as if the earth was breathing.

Almost bubbling.

And that was when he realized—*the floor of the pit wasn't solid.*

He squirmed, alarmed, his shoulders aching.

Because he realized something else. Though the floor of the pit wasn't solid, it wasn't liquid either. Halfway between. Viscous, it reminded him of quicksand, of muddy sinkholes in a swamp, of...

The ripple repeated itself, a wave that moved from one side to the other. Eddies.

More bubbles in the...

Slime, he decided. That was the only way to describe it. Slime. And the bubbles weren't caused by heat. No, there was something underneath.

In the green-brown slime that gave off an almost unbearable nauseating odor. Excrement, rotten food, decomposing animals, filth of every description, left to decay and seep and merge, to become an open cesspool, a semiliquid compost pit.

It lived.

It heaved and rippled and bubbled because there were things beneath its surface. Slugs and insects, worms and leeches.

And the bamboo cross began to descend. Thrashing his legs, trying to raise them above the heaving slime as long as he could, he wanted to scream. But he didn't—he wouldn't give Tay the satisfaction, and more, he had to shut off his mind, to quell his horror, to pretend he was a particle on the strand of a gossamer spider web, which wasn't real.

But the slime pit was real. He couldn't convince himself that it wasn't. Not enough time. Though he held up his legs, they slowly wearied with the gradual descent of the cross, and finally they drooped, his boots sinking into the slime, which had the consistency of pudding—green-brown pudding.

But his skin had not yet touched it, only his boots, so he couldn't feel it yet, could only stare in revulsion at the increasing ripples in the slime.

And all at once the bamboo cross dropped him knee-deep into the slime, and he felt its warm greasy squish around his legs. The cross dropped him farther. He felt sloshy mud around his groin. His privates shrank up close to his abdomen. Something small and squirmy tickled them.

And he suddenly was dropped shockingly to his neck. Things clung to his chest, sucking, stinging, biting.

In America, when he'd escaped from jail in that town, racing ahead of a posse into the mountains, using every trick and weapon he could think of to stay alive, he'd been forced to take cover in a mineshaft, indeed had been trapped in there, sealed in. Searching for another way out, he'd groped farther, deeper, into the mine, and at last had crawled sightless through a narrow passage, reaching a massively echoing, completely dark cavern. Where he stood waist-deep in guano, beetles nipping his skin. And then the bats had attacked him, swarming in a cluster around his head. He'd thought that he'd go insane, that the bat cave was the limit to what his mind could endure, that nothing worse could possibly ever happen to him.

But now he realized that he'd been wrong. In the heaving rippling slime, its stench so foul that it made him want to vomit, tiny creatures attached themselves to his body, nibbling, sucking. He peered up in desperation toward the top of the pit, where Tay watched with interest. Please! Rambo wanted to scream. Lift me out of here!

But Tay, grinning, waved farewell, gestured sharply behind him, and Rambo went all the way under.

Darkness.

It became unspeakable. Straining to hold his breath, feeling the slime rush into his ears, shoot up his nostrils, thrust at his lips, he scrunched his eyes shut. Pressure squeezed them inward, making him fear they would burst like grapes.

Down he went. Down. And his lungs burned, demanding air.

And his flesh cringed. Something licked the rim of one of his ears. Something burrowed up a nostril, spreading it. He wanted to snort, to expel the thing, but he feared that the effort would make him breathe reflexively. He'd gag. He'd open his mouth to cough. The slime would rush down his throat. The creatures would enter him. He'd drown.

His mind teetered. Can't take it any longer. Breathe. Have to. He struggled but couldn't free his arms to brush off the things on his chest, his neck, his mouth. And as his consciousness dwindled from oxygen starvation, his senses began shutting down. He moved as if in a nightmare, walking in place, going nowhere.

And then the slime pit and its creatures at last were no longer real. He'd achieved the ultimate Zen condition. The threshold of death.

The next thing, he had a vague sense of being jerked. He suddenly saw dim light beyond his closed eyelids. He felt the pressure on his chest decrease, slime dripping off him, air on his face. As the cross was hoisted abruptly up, he snorted, expelling the slug that had squirmed up his nose. He rubbed his ear against his shoulder, squashing a worm.

And breathed. Oh, Jesus, he could breathe.

"Another time?" Tay asked and grinned. "Or perhaps you'll answer the captain's questions now."

"Fuck you."

Beside Tay, Captain Vinh straightened in outrage.

"I should have warned you," Tay said. "The captain doesn't like foul language. I think I'll let you stay down there a little longer." He gestured to the guards.

The bamboo cross began to descend.

And peering down past the liver-colored, feeding, twitching leeches on his chest, Rambo knew that this time he'd die.

Or else go crazy.

Then answer their questions.

Like hell.

The Huey thundered into view across a bluff. Rambo tensed excitedly. American! They didn't leave me! They saw the soldiers back at the pickup site and went to get another chopper, to bring in reinforcements!

His boots dangled closer to the slime.

God dammit, hurry! If they drop me in here, you might not find me! I'll drown while you look for me!

The Huey grew, whump-whump-whumping louder, raising dust, bending bushes as it settled on the ground before the barracks. Any second now, Rambo knew, the Delta Force team would lunge out, rifles stuttering, machine guns strafing.

But why did they wait to touch down before they started to shoot?

Two roaring transport trucks sped jouncing through the compound's gate, their brakes grinding as they stopped a safe distance from the Huey. The backs of the trucks banged open. From one, fifteen Vietnamese soldiers jumped out.

From the other, still more soldiers.

But this second group was different.

And now Rambo understood why the Huey hadn't opened fire on the camp. *The soldiers from the second truck were Russians*. He recognized the insignia on their dark fatigues. They belonged to the elite Soviet Airborne Division.

Despair overcame him. The side door of the Huey slid open—the rotors whining slowly to a halt—and still more Russians appeared. Three Soviet Airborne Division soldiers.

And two lieutenants.

At once the Soviet group formed ranks and snapped to attention, saluting. The officers studied them critically, walking past them. As Rambo dangled, his arms in agony, over the pit, afraid that the Vietnamese would let him drop to be smothered, a part of him nonetheless couldn't help noticing the contrast in discipline—or lack of it—between the Vietnamese and the Soviets. And maybe Captain Vinh, with his immaculate uniform and his hand-washing gestures, wished that he was in a better army.

The Soviet officers were huge, their eyes utterly cold. They looked like walking doom.

Well, when you care enough, Rambo thought, you send the very best.

The officers stared in Rambo's direction and paused in disgust. One snapped an order to Captain Vinh, who though higher in rank approached them with quick respectful obedience.

Rambo couldn't hear what they said, but their gestures were angry, impatient. Captain Vinh nodded repeatedly, abruptly turning, shouting, "Sergeant, get the prisoner out of there!"

Tay knew enough not to argue. In fifteen seconds, Rambo stood—his legs wobbling, dripping slime—on the wonderfully solid ground beside the pit.

The Soviet officers came over, glanced up and down at Rambo, and wearily sighed.

"These people are so . . . crude," the blond said in English. "So vulgar." He noticed Rambo's knife in its sheath tucked into Sergeant Tay's belt and pulled it way. When he drew the blade, he nodded, admiring it. "This, on the other hand, is *not* crude."

Stepping closer, he traced the knife among what Rambo guessed must have been twenty huge blood-gorged leeches on his chest. With a casual gesture, the Soviet used the razor-sharp tip to sever one leech from the side of Rambo's neck, near the jugular. Rambo felt the steel against his vein. Like a master surgeon, the Soviet flicked the blade and threw the leech onto the ground.

"They lack compassion, I suspect," he said. "But we, however . . . I should introduce us. This is Lieutenant Yashin. I am Lieutenant Podovsk. I do not know who *you* are yet. But I will." He swung toward Tay and two other Vietnamese soldiers. "He stinks. Clean him up. Then take him . . ."—he pointed toward the middle barracks—". . . inside."

— 13 —

From the cave at the back of the camp, Banks stared through the bamboo bars, watching the Soviet officers stride away from the pit. The Vietnamese cut Rambo from the cross, threw a bucket of water over him, and dragged him away.

Behind Banks, a sickly prisoner wheezed. "We were pulling for you."

"Next time," Banks said.

"Sure." Without conviction. "Next time."

Another prisoner coughed. And again, hacking terribly. "Banks, were you ever tortured by the Russians?"

"Yeah."

"Well, what do you do? I mean, how do you keep from talking?"

Banks dismally stared toward the middle barracks. "Hope they kill you by mistake."

– 6 –

THE GRAVE

— I —

As two guards dragged him into a makeshift office in the barracks, Rambo felt a hand shove him hard from behind, smelled Sergeant Tay's foul breath, and lurched ahead.

Tay kicked at his ankle. As the guards let go, Rambo fell to the floor, reaching down to break his fall, scraping his hands.

The Soviets considered Tay's action, seeming to debate whether it, too, was vulgar.

"Not on the floor," Podovsk said. "The chair."

Tay gestured sharply. The guards yanked Rambo to his feet and shoved him onto the chair.

Keep cool, Rambo thought. It's not my turn yet. Just keep cool.

He glared at the Soviets, at Tay, at the guards. The room was small. A single bare bulk gleamed weakly from a dangling wire in the ceiling. On a metal desk, a microphone and a radio transmitter caught his attention.

"Thank you, Sergeant. You can go now," Podovsk said. "But leave one guard, please."

Tay squinted, frustrated. But he did what he was told. Fifteen seconds later, he and the second guard were gone.

Through the open window, Rambo saw that shadows had begun to form outside. The sun had passed its zenith.

Podovsk leaned against the metal table. Though as tall as his fellow officer, he was slighter of build. He wore wire-rimmed glasses, and with his intelligent, even sensitive, but finally calculating features, he resembled the stereotype of a bank president.

Yashin was another story. He had a broad slab of combat mustache, his hair cut short like a scrub brush. His features were as thick and broadly emphasized as Communist sculpture, suggesting a Nordic-Mongolian-Circassian heritage. A pine-tree patch on his shoulder showed his status as a *costune*, a cossack scout.

The silent moment ended as Podovsk approached, holding Rambo's knife, gesturing with it toward the scars on Rambo's chest. "I see you are no stranger to pain. Possibly you have been among my Vietnamese comrades before?" He waited. "No answer? No matter. Captain Vinh has already informed me that you once were a guest here. My question was only . . . how do you say it? . . . to break the ice." He found this very amusing. "Is that how you say it? Perhaps you will tell me your name. What harm can it cause? A name."

Rambo stared at the floor.

"Well," Podovsk said, "what a poor beginning for an intimate relationship. I assure you, by tomorrow . . . or the next day . . . you will tell me things you would not even tell a lover."

You're as goddamned ignorant as the people back home, Rambo thought. Lover? I don't *want* a lover.

And at once he thought, disturbed, about Co. Where *was* she? Had she managed to get away?

"But surely you know how senseless it is to resist," Podovsk said. "In the long run, pain is a poor substitute for intelligence. But let us begin. Are you working directly for the American government? Who are your local contacts? Where is your base? What arrangements were made to rescue the other prisoners? On and on. I have quite a list of questions. Will you tell me these things freely?"

Rambo glanced out the window toward the shadows as they lengthened.

"Of course, you won't," Podovsk said. "But as a moral

man, I felt compelled to ask. What you must understand is that we *have* to interrogate you. We have no other choice. We *will* find out the answers to my questions." He pointed Rambo's knife toward the chiseled features of his companion. "To Yashin here—he doesn't speak much, have you noticed?—you are a piece of meat, a laboratory animal, an experiment. To me, however"—Podovsk lightly tapped the knife against his uniform—"you are a comrade similar to myself, but different, of course, opposed to me by a matter of politics and fate. Such is life. I know your national loyalty prompted you—mistakenly, of course—to try to free your capitalist war criminals from this People's Republic. I can appreciate loyalty. Of whatever misguided sort. But this— your capture—this incident is—embarrassing. You must understand. We *must* have an explanation. After you answer my questions, I wish for you to use that radio and call back to your headquarters. Say you found no prisoners. Say your operation was a failure. Will you do this?"

Podovsk held up the microphone.

Rambo continued staring toward the lengthening shadows beyond the open window.

"Well," Podovsk said, "forgive me for boring you. Sometimes I get too eager. I get ahead of myself. Skip steps. Is that how you say it in America? Skip steps? Even that you won't answer? You wish to test your strength against pain. Very good. I sense that my friend has become impatient. I do not wish to frustrate him. Yashin, proceed."

The dark-haired mustached cossack scout stepped forward. Perhaps he smiled. It was hard to tell. What Rambo most noticed were the pliers he was holding.

— 2 —

Night.

Hearing the fart-burp-sputter of an ill-maintained Honda cycle, the guard in the sentry box at the gate glanced up from a black-market translation of a perfectly disgusting American trashy sex book and saw a headlight enlarging toward him. The cycle stopped before him—fart, burp, sputter—and the guard was able to distinguish a penis-arousing woman in a skintight dress and coolie hat who made a suggestion straight out of the book he was reading.

"Both ways?" He pretended to think about it, but he knew already what his answer would be. From pride, he even haggled about the price, but if she insisted, he decided he'd pay what she demanded. The local business was certainly improving. This girl on the cycle was so innocent-looking that the thought of having her—both ways, he remembered, though he wondered if he was capable of it—made him almost ejaculate in his uniform.

Yes, the night was certainly improving. He hadn't heard the prisoner who was being tortured in the barracks scream even once.

Soon though, he thought.

Yes, very soon.

The girl made an obscene gesture with her index finger into the encircled fingers of her other hand. She raised her eyebrows suggestively, and after he opened the gate to let her through, the sputter of her cycle receding, he cursed because of the stain at the crotch of his pants.

— 3 —

Feeling filthy merely because she'd talked to him, Co directed the noisy cycle—she'd stolen it from the nearby village—down the lane toward the barracks. Her tight dress and coolie hat as well were stolen. But despite that risk, she'd overcome a greater risk. The leering guard had let her through without a question about the leather tube, Rambo's quiver and disassembled bow, that she had strapped to the far side of the cycle. If the guard had asked, she would have told him that the tube contained supplies for doing it an exotic *third* way. But as she had expected, the guard didn't ask. He was too preoccupied by the inventive complexity she'd added to the first way.

She approached the faint lights in the barracks, her cycle sputtering, but despite its noise, she heard a sudden terrible scream.

Rambo's scream. And whatever had caused it, she knew— her heart beat angrily—that because he was her man the cause of his scream must have been beyond any human endurance. She would kill whoever had done this.

— 4 —

Rambo, standing upright, his wrists tied to metal bedsprings tilted against the wall, shuddered uncontrollably. There wasn't any will involved. His reaction was reflexive, spasmodic, like a frog attached to electrodes—as *he* had been attached to electrical wires that led back to a generator.

And that wasn't all. In the shadowy background, while Yashin impassively but with fascination worked the generator, Podovsk stirred Rambo's knife into a pot of gleaming blazing charcoal.

"It will be frustrating," Podovsk said, "if we cannot have a nice chat. Very *very* frustrating. Once again. My first question. What is your name?"

Bound to the upright springs, with a black metal plate the size of a paperback taped to his stomach, wires leading from it to the generator, Rambo stopped screaming as the current tapered off. Dripping water that Yashin had thrown on him, the liquid indistinguishable from the huge drops of sweat splashing onto the wet boards at his feet, he stared with the eyes of a frantic animal toward the night past the open window, toward the sweeping gleam of a sputtering cycle's headlight going past, and bit his lip, determined that next time he wouldn't scream.

"Not yet?" Podovsk asked. He left the knife in the blazing charcoal, turned angrily, and threw another pail of water over Rambo. "Again!" he told Yashin.

The current surged abruptly through his body, searing

the contact point beneath the black metal box on his stomach, filling the room with the stench of scorched flesh, convulsing his nerves and muscles at every extremity of his body. Shameful urine dribbled down his leg. He couldn't control his response.

Pride didn't matter. Discipline didn't matter. Pain was what mattered, and convulsively—despite how desperately hard he tried not to—he screamed and screamed till he thought that his vocal cords would burst.

The jolt of powerful current made the overhead light bulb flicker.

And Yashin turned the switch down.

Exhausted, Rambo hung from the bedsprings, heaving, shivering, gasping.

"Comrade," Podovsk said patiently, "surely you see how boring this is? I was scheduled for a leave. And you... There must be something you'd rather be doing." He patted at something in his jacket pocket. "Oh, yes, I almost forgot. Here. I have something you might be interested in."

He drew a piece of paper from his uniform, unfolded it and brought it over, holding it up to Rambo's pain-widened raging eyes.

"A transcript. The conversation between your helicopter pilot and his commander... code name Pack Leader... as the pickup crew abandoned you on that hill. Can you see through the sweat in your eyes to read it? No? Then let me do the favor of reading it for you. I'm sure you appreciate the effort from our overworked cryptography staff. With impressive commitment to their republic, they managed to intercept the message from your spy satellite and unscramble it."

Adjusting his glasses, Podovsk studied the unfolded paper.

"Hmm. Let me see here. Yes. 'Dragonfly... Wolf Den.' Colorful names. I assume they made sense to you. But let me get to the good part. 'Pack Leader, we have them in sight. Jesus, it's Rambo.' Aside from the anti-republic pseudo-religious epithet . . . Well, you must realize now that I knew your name all along. Rambo. And I knew the answers to my other questions as well. So you see, the pain you're so admirably enduring has been needless. You could have saved all of us a great deal of time and effort. But I mustn't interrupt myself. Let me continue with the transcript. Another good part. 'Christ, he's got one. He's got one of ours.' The translation is free, but you get—as you say—the gist. And this is the best part. From Wolf Den. From Pack Leader. 'Abort the operation immediately. Return to base camp.'"

With exaggerated grace, Podovsk moved the paper close to Rambo's eyes.

"'Abort. Return to base.' My, my. Correct me if I'm wrong. It seems they intentionally abandoned you. On direct orders. And these are the people you protect with your silence?" Podovsk sounded astonished. "With your pain? How misguided can loyalty be? Don't you think it would be better . . . would make you *feel* better . . . if you got even with them? Speak to them on the radio. Denounce them. Let the world know the crimes they've committed."

Podovsk's smile was friendly, appealing. "Then we can give you medical attention. Decent food. A chance to sleep. Not here in this pigsty, of course. In the excellent hospital at our base in Cam Ranh Bay."

Rambo looked away from him, toward the night at the open window.

Podovsk sighed. "Not yet. Very well. You may continue screaming if you wish. There is nothing embarrassing about it. In this room, there is no shame."

Podovsk snapped his fingers. Yashin turned the knob on the generator, and as Rambo felt the sudden excruciating surge of current through his ravaged twitching nervous system, he did indeed scream.

Long and hard.

And Podovsk screamed with him. "Yes!" He was sexually excited, his eyes wide, his groin bulging. "Yes! You must scream! You must! There is no shame!"

— 5 —

Outside in the night, it began to rain. As Rambo's drawn-out, hoarse, ever-louder scream shrilled across the compound, echoing horribly off the bluffs, making soldiers turn toward the middle barracks, a gentle mist became a pleasant drizzle, sweetly pelting the ground, hissing through leaves, drumming hollowly on the corrugated-metal roofs of the buildings. The unseen clouds unloaded, and the drizzle became a full, heavy, thunderous downpour, bringing with it a breeze that seemed almost cool compared to the cloying sultry stillness that had preceded it. Branches thrashed. Sentries sought cover. The wallop of rain on the metal obscured Rambo's scream.

And in a room in the barracks to the right, Co withdrew her knife from the renal artery in the back of the soldier she had just killed, removing her hand from his mouth, letting his twitching body drop to the floor. His head whacked hard against wood. Ignoring his blood on her stolen provocative dress, she used the knife to shorten the hem, cutting a strip off so her knees showed, then making a slit halfway up her thigh. She grabbed the dead soldier's AK-47 where it leaned against the wall, shut off the light, and opened the door.

Outside the rain fell so thick and heavy that she couldn't see the guard tower.

Good. The guard up there would not be able to see her either.

She cautiously shut the door behind her and, suddenly

drenched by rain, hurriedly crept toward the Honda scooter she'd stolen, groping for the quiver and the disassembled bow that she'd hidden in bushes beside the barracks. Taking a screwdriver from a pouch on the scooter, she put the bow together as she'd seen her man do it.

Her man. She jerked up, frightened. But not for herself. Because despite the thunderous rain she could nonetheless hear that Rambo's terrible scream had stopped.

She bristled with rage. Her man. If they'd killed him . . . !

— 6 —

Lightning crackled past the window, the night for an instant day. Then darkness returned. The rain persisted.

Rambo hung limply from the bedsprings against the wall. His face was gaunt from pain. His muscles sagged from the devastation of convulsions. He wasn't sure how much more damage he could take and still survive.

Podovsk seemed to share his thought, approaching concerned.

Rambo mustered enough strength to raise his head. His vision was misty, but he managed to see Podovsk's mouth widen in a grin.

"Good. You are still alive. Impressive. You are strong. The strongest I have ever encountered." Podovsk's grin dissolved. "But the fact is, you are also nearly dead. And for what? Is your life worth protecting the men who betrayed you? I see no sense in this. Make the radio call. Yes? Please?"

The door banged open. As Rambo shifted his gaze and Podovsk spun, a dripping figure lunged in from the rain.

No, Rambo realized that his blurred eyes deceived him. Not one figure. Two. One man shoving another ahead of him. Sergeant Tay pushing Banks, controlling him with a thin wire that Tay had twisted sharply around his prisoner's neck. Tay gave it a needless jerk. Banks gagged.

"You see how friendly I am," Podovsk told Rambo. "I've arranged a reunion." He nodded to Yashin...

... who left the generator, motioned for Tay to step aside, and threw Banks brutally against the wall to Rambo's left.

Groaning, Banks collapsed, a heap on the floor.

"To talk," Podovsk said, "to obey would be much easier. Less pain all the way around. Or soon you will see."

Again he nodded to Yashin, who this time removed Rambo's knife, it's blade glowing, from the coals. With the knife held up like a beacon, Yashin approached Rambo and brought the red-hot blade slowly, relentlessly, toward Rambo's eyes.

The heat, the glow, made Rambo try to turn his head.

But with his other hand, Yashin viciously clutched Rambo's chin and forced him to look at the blade. Its burning glow reflected off Yashin's eyes.

"He has a memento for you of this occasion," Podovsk said.

At once Yashin pressed the molten tip against Rambo's left cheek. Flesh hissed. The smell of scorched meat filled the room. Rambo thrashed in agony, somehow not screaming, imagining the seared, triangular, smoking burn mark.

"Make the radio call?" Podovsk asked. "No? Not yet? Shove it in his eye."

As Rambo tried to jerk his head back protectively, banging it against the bedsprings, Yashin inexplicably stepped back.

And Rambo suddenly understood. Podovsk hadn't meant

his eye! No, he meant Banks!

Sergeant Tay jerked the prisoner's head up. Yashin stepped closer.

"If your life means nothing," Podovsk said, "perhaps the life of your friend does."

Yashin stopped in front of Banks. While Tay held the prisoner's head firm, Yashin began to move the glowing tip of the knife in a circle. Gradually the circle narrowed. The red-hot blade moved closer to Banks's right eye.

"You will," Podovsk said. "You *will* talk."

And closer.

Rambo thrashed, desperate.

"Yes," Podovsk said, his face flushed with excitement again. *"You will."*

The blade was about to pierce Banks's eye. "Don't say anything!" Banks yelled. "Let the bastards do what they want!"

But the blade moved ever closer. Shaking, raging, Rambo imagined how the eye would pop, steamy liquid bursting out.

"Yes?" Podovsk asked.

And Rambo, sagging, nodded.

Yashin stepped back with the knife. Tay let go of Banks, who fell hard on the floor.

Podovsk smiled. "Excellent. We're finally making progress. I applaud your wisdom. Only a fool dies for a lost cause. Or allows a friend to die."

He stepped to the metal table and turned on the radio transmitter. "Our specialists have determined the frequency. But I trust you know the proper transmit codes. Yes?"

Again Rambo nodded, furious, sullen.

"Don't do it!" Banks yelled. "These bastards won't let us—!"

"Shut up!" Tay kicked him in the face, splitting his lips, knocking him unconscious.

Rambo winced.

And forced himself to look away.

Podovsk picked up the microphone. "You will state your

name. That you've been captured as a spy. You will state that the mission was a failure and all missions will fail. Tell them not to attempt such hostile aggression again. Denounce their war crimes. Understand?"

Rambo nodded again.

"Do it now!" Podovsk turned on the microphone and held it close to Rambo's pain-twisted lips.

Rambo struggled to breathe. For the first time in this room, he spoke. His voice broke, crusty, hoarse. "Two-twenty, fifty-six. Lone Wolf . . ." He had to swallow to make his voice work. He coughed. ". . . to Wolf Den. Receive."

— 7 —

In the hangar, Trautman stared bleakly at the map of Thailand, Laos . . .

. . . and Vietnam. Where Rambo had been abandoned. Where only God knew what hell he was going through right now.

Or if he was even still alive.

Around him, technicians and military personnel were hurriedly packing equipment, loading crates into the Peregrine jet and the Agusta chopper. Other choppers would soon be arriving. "Pack up, move out," Murdock had ordered. And on the double, they were obeying.

But this isn't over, Trautman thought. When I get back to the States, I'll nail Murdock's ass to a wall.

Amid the noise that the technicians made, packing equipment, Trautman suddenly heard a faint hoarse voice from the radio.

"Wolf Den. This is . . . two-twenty, fifty-six . . . Lone Wolf . . . to Wolf Den. Do you read me? Over."

At once Trautman's stomach burned. He slammed down the cup of untasted coffee that he'd been holding and swung toward the radio console.

He wasn't the only one who jerked to attention. Technicians, military personnel, Ericson, Doyle, they all suddenly froze, snapping their gaze toward the radio.

"Two-twenty, fifty-six, we read you, Lone Wolf!" the radio operator blurted into the microphone. "Where are you? Over."

From the corner of his vision, Trautman noticed a blur of movement. Glancing that way, he saw Murdock appear at his office doorway.

"What the hell's going on?" Murdock asked. "Why aren't you people packing?"

"Sir, it's Rambo," the radio operator said. "He's reporting in."

Murdock actually flinched. "Rambo? No, it . . . That's impossible."

— 8 —

Sweating, his arms still tied to the bedsprings, Rambo swallowed again. Hateful, he glared at the microphone Podovsk held to his mouth.

A voice broke through the static coming from the radio. *"We read you, Lone Wolf. What is your position? Over."*

Rambo didn't respond.

The voice became more urgent. *"What's your position, Lone Wolf? Over."*

Podovsk whispered, "Your position will be death if you do not answer."

Yashin approached, making circles with the knife.

— 9 —

Trautman couldn't bear waiting any longer. Impatient, he snatched the microphone from the radio operator. "John, this is Trautman! Where the hell are you?"

Static crackled.

"Johnny, come in!"

More static. A groan. A hoarse voice—

Rambo's voice, Trautman thought excitedly. But the weakness and strain in it troubled him.

—said one word only.

Two syllables.

"Murdock."

The hangar became even more still. Technicians frowned at each other. In the background, Ericson—seemingly indifferent—broke the frozen tableau by reaching for a beer.

But Murdock stiffened, his face a welter of conflicting emotions.

Nervous. Puzzled. Self-conscious as everybody turned to him.

"He's here." Trautman's eyes narrowed as he shoved the microphone over.

And Murdock gripped it apprehensively. He glanced

around, everybody staring at him, and forced a grin to his face—a shit-eating grin, Trautman thought.

"Rambo." Murdock sounded delighted. "This is Pack Leader. We're glad you're alive. Where are you? Give us your position, and we'll come and get you. Over."

Trautman wanted to puke in disgust.

Static. *"Murdock..."*

The silence lengthened.

"...I'm coming for you."

Someone inhaled sharply.

Murdock's face lost its color. His grin dissolved. He lowered the microphone.

His voice shook. "...Christ."

— 10 —

"You...!" Podovsk's rage was too great for him to choose a word to express it. His eyes widening grotesquely behind his glasses, he swung the microphone back to whip it at Rambo's face, abruptly changed his direction, and lunged toward the generator next to the radio.

With a savage thrust, he turned the dial.

And Rambo felt the sudden surge, the vicious jolt of current, the overwhelming pain as his body jerked, horribly convulsing, slamming him back against the bedsprings.

He screamed.

He kept on.

He couldn't stop.

And finally reached the dark in himself. The deepest

level. It was partly in his mind, partly in his chest, mostly in his soul. A black pit incredibly compressed, compacted under pressure, held in stasis by rigid force.

And as Podovsk turned the dial even higher, the current making Rambo shudder faster, convulse more disgustingly, shriek even louder, the black pit exploded.

— || —

With his hand on the generator's dial, turning it ever higher, watching this American pig jerk spastically against the bed-springs, Podovsk suddenly realized that something was wrong.

Possibly *very* wrong. His experience had taught him that the jolt of current was not yet high enough to account for the prisoner's increased violent agitation. The shriek was more fierce than Podovsk would have predicted.

Indeed, to put it mildly, the prisoner seemed to be going berserk. His body was an out-of-control machine, lashing, tearing at the bedsprings. His scream, having risen to a shriek, was now a ferocious howl. He sounded like an animal. A horribly frightening animal.

Unnerved, Podovsk left the generator, its dial turned up. Almost hypnotized by the furious deafening spectacle, he approached the obscenely shuddering prisoner, whose howl had become more feral. The springs began to twist, creaking, warping under the disgusting American's frenzied assault.

Podovsk realized too late that the current was merely the

stimulus. The American was adding to it, propelled into such a rage that—

Welds broke. Springs popped. Podovsk took a reflexive step backward.

Not soon enough. He saw a hand, suddenly freed, shoot toward him like a grappling hook.

He stood in a pool of water that had dripped from the prisoner. And felt the current—no!—seize him. Transmitted through the prisoner, it jolted his heart. It made his limbs shake like a puppet. It made his penis become erect. And ejaculate. And he felt the shaking hasplike fingers tear at his throat.

— 12 —

In a rage, Rambo threw him toward the generator. The Russian's body tangled in the wires that led to the black box on his chest. Wires snapped loose. The current mercifully stopped. As Podovsk hit the table, toppling the generator, Rambo ignored him, breaking his other arm free, swinging toward Yashin, who lunged with the knife.

But Yashin wasn't quick enough. Ducking toward the floor, Rambo grabbed the microphone that Podovsk had dropped. He drove it up, hard, cracking Yashin's jaw, blood and jagged teeth flying, propelling him across the room.

But that still left Sergeant Tay and the guard, both of them raising their rifles. He couldn't get to both of them, widely separated, before...

Their fingers tensed on triggers.

And the floor exploded upward, splinters flying. The blast threw Rambo back against the bedsprings. Reflexively he raised his arms to protect his eyes from shrapnel. Smoke whirled around him. The stuttering blast of an AK-47 rebounded off the walls. And as the smoke cleared, he saw Co leaping up from the hole in the floor, pivoting her rifle around the room. Podovsk and Yashin lay unconscious, bleeding. The guard was dead on the floor. And Tay was gone, the door open, angry shouts alerting the guards outside as rain cascaded past the entrance.

Lightning flashed, followed by thunder.

Rambo grabbed his knife from Yashin's stupefied grasp. Co threw him the bow and the quiver.

And as if they had trained together for months, he sprinted with Co toward a window. Co reached it first, leaping out. And then . . .

— 13 —

As lightning gleamed again, a spotlight arced through the downpour. They frantically raced through mud toward the camp's perimeter. Seeing the light veer in their direction, Rambo halted just long enough to nock an arrow onto the bow, draw hurriedly, and shoot. With a thrum and hiss, the arrow left the bow. If its vanes had been made from feathers and not from plastic, as they were, the arrow would have had its guidance mechanism softened by the rain and its trajectory deflected. But designed as it was, the arrow streaked directly on course, shattering the arc light.

The darkness returned.

But lightning illuminated them. Muzzles flashed, automatic weapons rattling, bullets whunking into the forest behind them.

Co fired controlled repeated bursts in return.

They hurried farther. Another searchlight came on, speeding toward them, and this time as lightning gleamed, it streaked down like a blazing missile and struck one barracks. The entire camp, the searchlight, even the lights in the buildings, flickered, dimmed, went bright, and died.

The darkness was absolute.

But tracer bullets pierced it, their phosphorus-coated tips whipping toward the jungle, gleaming, beautiful, deadly. The stutter of gunfire was louder than the thunder that suddenly shook the encampment.

They reached the loose rolls and barbed wire. Rambo grabbed a strand, lifting, his hand bleeding as barbs cut deeply into his flesh.

Co crawled under.

Then realizing a better way, Rambo lay with his back on the mud, shoved the bow beneath the wire, lifted the bow above him, raising the wire, and squirmed beneath the barbs.

They scrambled toward the second fence. As tracer bullets blazed ghostly past them, Co halted, raised her rifle, and shot at a wooden post where the wires were attached. The post splintered, barbed wires snapping, whipping with a ping to the right and left.

And as they charged through the opening, Rambo heard bullets make a thunk-thunk-thunking sound into trees ahead of him, bark exploding, leaves disintegrating into confetti.

But they were out.

"You're amazing," Rambo said as he raced through the undergrowth.

She was furious at him for wasting his breath to speak. *"Di di mau!* Go! Go!"

The tracer bullets pivoted to their left, shredding another part of the forest.

And she *was* amazing, he thought as he ran. She really was.

Podovsk's nose and mouth dripped blood as he raged from the middle barracks. Even more furious than he'd been when Rambo had tricked him with the radio, he scowled at the chaos of lightning, tracer bullets, thunder, frantic shadows, and contradictory shouts.

In a blaze of lightning, he noticed Sergeant Tay pointing this way and that, a sadistic idiot who deserved every moment his commanders made him stay in this shithole.

And where was Captain Vinh, the genteel Captain Vinh, who felt above it all, who kept his uniform immaculate, and dreamed of being stationed in Hanoi with a subordinate who'd do all his work for him while Vinh diddled girl friends in his sampan in the harbor?

Probably in his room, afraid of getting his uniform wet. Mother of Lenin!

Podovsk charged, his boots squishing in the mud, the blood on his face trickling off in the rain, and angrily grabbed Tay by his collar. "Find him! Unless you want me to throw you into the slime pit, find him! Now!"

Tay blinked in shock.

At once Podovsk felt someone shouldering past him. Yashin. A blaze of lightning showed that, when Yashin opened his mouth to speak, his front teeth were broken, jagged.

"And when you find him..." Yashin shuddered with fury.

Amazing, Podovsk thought. He almost never speaks.

"And when you find him, kill him!"

Tay—his voice communicating utter terror—barked orders at his men, pointing toward the forest.

And as the Vietnamese rushed away, Podovsk thought: Why am I mucking around with these amateurs? I've got my own squad.

He turned. In another flash of lightning, he saw his Soviet soldiers standing in military formation, their faces rigid, stark, rifles poised, ready for orders.

Years ago, Podovsk had seen a black-market American film called *M*A*S*H,* starring Donald Sutherland and Elliott Gould, typical imperialists. The plot depicted a U.S. surgical team in Korea during the American invasion. At one point, the principal characters had been sent to Japan to operate on the sick heart of the son of an American general. In sweaty fatigues, they had entered a hospital with no concern about the germs they brought with them to contaminate the patients and, eager to play the bourgeois elitist unproductive game of golf, they'd announced to a justly indignant nurse, "We're the pros from Dover." Whatever *that* meant. "We mean to crack this kid's chest and be on the links by two o'clock."

Selfish. Arrogant.

But clearly confident that they were the best.

Professionals.

This thought rushed for less than a second through Podovsk's mind as he strained to understand how he felt about his squad.

Surveying them, he nodded. Yes, why did he need Tay and the genteel Capital Vinh and these inferior fools?

He had his pros from Dover.

Confident, he started barking commands.

And noticed that Yashin was already rushing with two other men toward the helicopter.

— 15 —

His heart pounding excitedly, thrilled to be free, Rambo zigzagged through the dark of the forest, Co scrambling next to him. They reached a slope and clawed at slippery tree roots, struggling through the rain up the muddy incline, slipping, sagging, straining harder, reaching the top.

Abruptly he stiffened. He heard the chugging roar of helicopter rotors, and turning, he frowned as two powerful searchlights rose from the forest, sweeping back and forth, their shafts competing with a burst of lightning to determine which was brighter. And the roar of the engine competed with the subsequent roll of thunder.

Crouching on the hill, Rambo tensely scanned the dark rain-obscured forest below him.

And saw handlights searching, broken by trees, as they swept in one direction, then another.

Shouts down there.

Frantic gunfire. A pig squealed. Stopped.

The helicopter, massively outlined as lightning blazed, tilted in the gusting rain. It must have been piloted by a maniac. Only the most obsessed, determined, outraged of pilots would dare to risk flying the chopper in this storm to search after them.

And Rambo suddenly knew who it was.

The silent one.

The cossack.

Yashin . . .

— 16 —

. . . clutched the Huey's controls, working the rudder pedals, trying to compensate as the huge chopper tilted from yet another powerful gust. The chopper's responses were sluggish. He concentrated, managed to steady it, and angrily ignored the risk of flying above the forest in this storm. A slight miscalculation in the dark, a too-strong surge of wind, and the Huey's landing skids could easily snag in a treetop, flip the chopper over, and kill him in an atomizing ball of flame.

But the risk didn't matter. Only the prisoner mattered and whoever had helped him. His mind retained a hate-producing photograph of the prisoner swinging the microphone at him. As the trauma of the blow to his mouth began to lessen, as the pain of his missing front teeth throbbed, growing to excruciating intensity, he spat out blood and cursed. He felt as if broken glass had been rammed beneath his gums. He strained not to miss the slightest movement down there as the Huey's searchlights scanned the forest. A pig burst out of bushes, two Vietnamese soldiers chasing it till they realized that it wasn't the prisoner. Tay suddenly appeared, shaking them with fury, shoving them up a slope. Rain lashed the chopper's canopy. Speeding onward, rising with the slope, Yashin saw other soldiers scrambling, raising their hands to protect their eyes from the Huey's searchlights. Now Yashin sped even higher, scanning the top of the slope. Despite the whumping roar of the chopper, he heard thunder. And abruptly realized that it wasn't thunder

176

at all. An explosion! And pivoting the Huey, staring down at the glare of his searchlights, he saw . . .

. . . legs. One hanging in a bush. The other in a puddle. Continuing to scan his searchlights, he saw the body that the legs had belonged to. A Vietnamese soldier flat on his back. Eyes wide. Mouth open. Screaming soundlessly in shock, then slumping unconscious, possibly dying. Several soldiers gathered around. Wiser ones rushed forward. Tay appeared, shouting at those who hung back.

And Yashin pivoted the chopper again toward the top of the slope, choosing the only draw that led down toward the blackness of a valley. In the prisoner's place, he thought, I'd take that draw, that valley. I'd want room to maneuver. I'd want to avoid getting trapped against these cliffs.

And I can reach the valley much sooner.

As Yashin fought another surge of wind, urging the Huey down the draw through the dark and the storm, he breathed deeply with excited anticipation.

Yes, when the American leaves that draw, I've got a surprise for him.

Because when the Huey had been captured from the South Vietnamese Army in 1975, its liberators had been delighted to find a bonus. One of the superguns that the Americans had so enjoyed using.

Yes, Yashin thought, I've got a dragon.

— 17 —

Gasping, exhausted, Co slumped against a boulder in the draw, hunkering low in bushes, ready to squirm even farther into the dark of the storm-tossed undergrowth if the helicopter's searchlights veered this way.

Rambo stopped and knelt beside her, breathing hard. He raised his face to the rain, filling his mouth, terribly thirsty, swallowing. His ordeal at the camp had sapped his strength, drained his energy. His body ached in every joint and muscle. The only thing that had kept him running was the instinct to save his life.

And his sense of release, his exuberance in being free.

But though he desperately wanted to *keep* his freedom, he knew that if he ran to the point of total exhaustion he wouldn't be able to defend himself.

Besides, he had to think of Co. She had saved his life. And if she wanted to rest, by God, that's what they'd do.

"I haven't had a chance," he said, still catching his breath.

"To what?"

"To thank you."

"Yeah," she said proudly, "you get ass kicked without me."

He had to laugh, agreeing. "We're a pretty good team. How'd you blow up the floor?"

"With"—she pointed toward his quiver—"the explosive and detonators."

Lightning gleamed. As the chopper's searchlights descended far below them, its whump-whump-whump diminishing through the dark toward what presumably was a valley, he ducked reflexively into the bushes with her.

"You look like hell," Co said. "Wounds infected."

He knew it, but he shrugged to try to reassure her.

"No, you hurt bad. Need medicine. Doctor. I get worried. Maybe you not so in-vul-nerabo as you think."

He thought about it. "Maybe not."

"What you do now? You try go across Laos? Reach Thailand?"

"Yeah." His anger flared. "I've got some business there."

"And then you go America?"

"It's hard to . . . After my business, I might not be too welcome there."

"But if you do go . . . ?"

"What?"

"You take me with you? Rambo, I give you one more chance. Get married."

"You don't know me."

"Know you well enough. You take me United States. I see my son, Nguyen. See my brother. Maybe use degree, teach economics. Buy Cadillac. Watch 'Dallas.'"

Despite the circumstances, he had to laugh.

But in another gleam of lightning, he saw the urgent need on her face.

He sobered. "You saved my life. You want to go to America?" He nodded sharply. "You got it."

"You make good choice."

"That's me. A helluva guy."

He swung toward angry shouts up the slope from them. As the glare of handlights swept through the underbrush, he murmured, "We'd better get moving."

But as they scurried through the dark gusting rain, heading farther down the draw, he again felt distressed by the skill with which these soldiers were tracking him. Yesterday, when he'd been followed from the river, he'd used various tricks to hide his trail and slow down the soldiers. Wading up streams so there'd be no footprints. Leaving sharp-staked boobytraps that would spring up from a gully and impale a pursuer. Spreading branches and leaves across sinkholes, disguising them, so they'd trap a hunter.

But whatever he did, it hadn't been enough. The soldiers had continued relentlessly after him.

Someone back there was a damned good tracker.

Maybe the best Rambo had ever been up against.

— 18 —

Tay resisted the urge to smile. Yes, there, he thought, aiming his handlight toward the rain-soaked ground. Despite the deepening puddles, he saw the vague impression, the faintest suggestion of a footprint. None of the fools he commanded would have noticed it or have understood it for what it was.

But *he* did. Just as, despite the rain and the narrow beam of his handlight, he noticed the barely bent stem of a rubber leaf ten paces farther on. In the rain, the stem was so supple that it hadn't broken when the American and his helper had rushed by. Instead, it had snapped back almost into place, leaving hardly any sign that someone had passed. Except for the pinched, wrinkled spot halfway down its stem. Yes, someone had passed here, all right.

And now Tay saw a patch of dead fallen leaves where someone had slipped. To the fools who hurried behind him, the patch would have looked no different from any other. But to him—he finally did allow himself to grin, proud, excited—to him, the exposed earth in the middle of the patch had a shallower puddle than a similar indentation beneath a bush beside it. The rain had not had a chance to fill it. And only one thing could have caused that. Someone had passed here recently and exposed that depression in the ground.

Recently, yes. Tay's smile became a rictus of hate. *Very* recently. Not long now.

Not far. And then, as the cossack had ordered, the American would be killed.

But—Tay's rictus broadened as he hurried, scanning the trail with his handlight—killed slowly. In delicious detail.

Because I never got a chance to finish flaying him.

And I'll use his knife.

When Rambo had escaped from the prison camp the first time, years before, Tay had pursued him madly through the forest for three long days. Bad enough that the American had eluded him. Worse that the American had been sick, an easy opponent.

At least, so Tay's commander had thought. The insults still echoed fiercely in Tay's unforgiving memory. And when word had come back that the American had reached America and even been awarded his country's highest medal for his escape, the insults had become more extreme, the loss of face almost too much for him to bear. He'd been demoted to the rank of private. He'd been further punished by orders that required him to remain on this hellish prison-guard duty.

But he'd been patient.

Diligent.

He'd worked his way back up to the rank of sergeant. And more important, determined not to let his disgrace ever be repeated, he'd become obsessed with the techniques of tracking someone. In every region where he was stationed—and there were many regions; these prisoners were moved around a great deal—he'd sought out the expert trackers in all the local villages. He'd forced them to teach him everything they knew.

Because, by Buddha, he would never lose face like that again. If another prisoner ever escaped, and if Tay was the soldier in charge of finding him, *that prisoner would be found*.

Maybe then he'd be able to redeem himself sufficiently to be given a transfer. Perhaps even down to Ho Chi Minh City, which during the war had been called Saigon and had been the utmost symbol of decadence. After this seemingly infinite horrible tour of duty, he wanted a *lot* of decadence.

And as he saw another sign, and yet another, of two people who'd raced through the rain down this dark draw ahead of him, he almost started laughing with sadistic glee.

Because the American was to blame for his ruined career.

And now the American was giving him a chance to make it a success.

For an eerie moment, as lightning blazed, followed by explosive thunder, he thought he was back in the war. But though his country had won, he had not.

And now in a resumption of his own private war, he would have a chance to win as his country had.

— 19 —

The rain persisted, but the night had become false dawn. As Rambo raced through bushes, he saw their outlines in the dusk. He noticed the silhouettes of trees. He saw the tangle of the forest.

Running next to him, Co looked alarmed in his direction. They didn't need to talk about it. Now that the dark was dispersing, they'd lost their advantage. The noises of the soldiers charging through the bushes behind them were too close as it was. If the soldiers managed to see them...

Objects became even clearer, the rain a drab clear gray. Rambo's vision extended to ten feet ahead of him. Fifteen. Twenty.

And as he burst from trees into a clearing fifty yards wide—now he could see even that far—he almost stopped. His shoulder blades shrank.

His spine tingled. Seeing the open space, threatened by it, he wanted to dart back into the trees, to use them for cover and veer around the clearing.

But Co was already a third of the way across it.

Unwilling to separate, Rambo raced after her.

But with sudden horror, he realized that the whump-whump-whump of the Huey was roaring louder, coming this way.

He shouted to Co to come back. She didn't listen, half-way across now. Committed, he ran even harder toward her.

The Huey was suddenly there.

A deeper, fuller, louder roar burst out of it. A column of orange fire erupted toward the clearing as gattling-gun barrels rotated in a blur.

Oh, Jesus, Rambo thought.

The Huey had a dragon.

— 20 —

Streaking toward the clearing, his eyes focused narrowly on the scrambling figures, one of which was unmistakably the American, Yashin rigidly gripped the Huey's controls, dipping, feeling his stomach rise, concentrating so hard that he bit down on his bottom lip . . .

Only to be reminded — excitement had blurred his pain — that he had no teeth with which to bite down. Where his teeth should have been, brittle fragments lanced his mouth.

And with savage anger, he continued to press the firing button on the dragon.

He'd waited, pretending to search the valley, his actual target the exit from the draw.

He'd been clever.

Yes, and oh so patient, waiting for the figures to emerge.

And now he would have his revenge.

— 21 —

The dragon.

Rambo had seen it in action many times. No matter how often, he'd never gotten used to it, had never adjusted to its almost incomprehensible power. As fear made his legs pump harder, as he narrowed the distance to Co, the ground to his right seemed to blow away. Jesus.

Jesus. The noise was awesome. One of the most devastating antipersonnel weapons ever devised, the General Electric ("Progress Is Our Most Important Product") M-134 Minigun fired 6,000 7.62 rounds per minute. Six *thousand* of them.

But that was only part of its effect. Its designers—not satisfied with overkill—had also added fireworks. Every fifth round was a tracer. A barrage from the gun created the impression of a solid shaft of fire stretching from the gunship toward the ground.

And its sound wasn't the rattle or the stutter of an ordinary machine gun. Instead, it boomed a continuous roll of thunder, as if a prehistoric monster—able to breathe fire—had belched long and hard.

And that was why soldiers had ironically called it Puff, the Magic Dragon.

In a solid blast, the clearing seemed to disintegrate. Wet grass whipped up, puréed as if in a Cuisinart gone insane. Chunks of mud became shoulder-high stinging dust.

And Co kept running.

Rambo reached her, sprinting with her toward the trees on the other side.

The Huey streaked over, whump-whump-whumping, pivoting in as narrow a radius as seemed possible.

And again Puff belched its thunderous flames.

Ahead of Rambo, trees became kindling. Leaves were pulverized. Bushes turned into mist. The tracer bullets streaked past him like a whooshing orange ray that stripped vines from rocks and then blasted the rocks into clouds.

But Rambo reached the trees as the Huey once more streaked overhead. Even in the rain, it cast a horrid shadow. Whump-whump-whump!

But Puff would be back. Puff would burp and reduce the edge of the forest to sawdust. He had to keep running, to seek the deeper protection of the forest.

He suddenly realized.

Co was no longer next to him.

Not even close behind him.

She was back at the edge of the clearing.

And turning, dreading, he saw her sprawled with her head face down among bushes, the rest of her out in the clearing.

Whump-whump-whump!

The Huey pivoted, returning.

No! His heart pounding so hard that he heard it behind his ears, he raced back, seeing the blood on her clothes, the terrible indentations in her back. And as he hung the bow and quiver around his shoulders, lifting her, his hands around her chest and her thighs, he felt Co's blood seep through his fingers, stringy flesh projecting through them.

No! He wanted to scream. Couldn't waste time. He had to get her away before...

Burp!

The dragon strafed the edge of the forest, looming directly toward the spot where Rambo had entered, and he'd never run so frantically, so hard, charging through the rain, past trees, through bushes, trying to put as much distance . . .

The bullets never touched him, but the force of their impact against the buffering trees behind him stung splinters against his back.

And threw him to the ground.

Over Co.

And he rammed his elbows into the ground so his weight wouldn't knock the breath from her.

His elbows—though the ground was softened by rain—were scraped raw.

Twisting over her, staying flat, he dragged her farther into the forest, mud clinging to him, blood trickling, rain—dispersed by the branches overhead—spraying over him.

And finally stopped.

Puff was impotent now. Puff could never breathe fire this deep into the forest.

Whump-whump-whump!

The Huey hovered out there, sounding frustrated, angry.

He cradled her in his arms, her blood seeping over his waist and legs.

She blinked at him, shuddering. "Wa-ky number one. Rambo."

He rocked her, trying frantically to send his life into her, to will her to live. Anguish contorted his face till its muscles cramped and ached. "Not Rambo. *John.* My name is *John!*"

Her cloudy eyes peered up at him, puzzled. "It doesn't hurt. Why?" She strained to breathe. "Why doesn't it . . . ?"

Feeling her body sag in his arms, he started to sob.

"You good man . . . John. Good. Helluva . . . Not forget me?"

"No. Believe it."

And she was . . .

. . . dead. He'd cradled too many dead soldiers, buddies, friends, not to recognize the weight that a soul left after it soared from the body.

Meat.
No longer beautiful.
No longer dignified.
Meat.
Dead meat.
And with all the power in his body, he screamed.

— 22 —

"Do you really think you can threaten me, Colonel?"

Pacing in fury, Trautman glared down at Murdock, who—adjusting his glasses—flipped through several status reports on his desk and tilted the tensor lamp so he could see them better.

"I want the rescue team ready to go in one hour," Trautman said flatly.

"You want . . . ?" Murdock peered up as if he couldn't believe what he'd heard. "Colonel, you're risking your career, your reputation, even your family's security." He took off his glasses and blinked in amazement. "Do you honestly believe that any one person is worth that much?"

"Yes," Trautman said, straightening. "Yes, I do. Rambo is."

Murdock's mouth opened. For a moment, he was speechless. "I'm giving you a direct order to withdraw from this project."

"Do I get the rescue team," Trautman said, even more furious, wanting to strangle the son of a bitch, "or do I have to go over your head?"

Murdock somehow found this amusing. He actually

laughed. "You don't seem to understand. *I'm* in charge here. You're just a cog." He gestured toward Ericson and Doyle. *"We're* the machine." Abruptly bored, he said, "Ericson, I want him placed under arrest. He's not to leave the base."

Not only Ericson but Doyle as well stood, responding to Murdock's orders. Doyle, the truly crazy one, had his hand on his holstered .45.

Trautman stared at the half-holstered weapon.

And slowly turned, barely able to restrain himself, toward Murdock. "Rambo never had a chance, did he?"

"Well," Murdock said and shrugged, "like you said, Colonel, he went home."

— 23 —

In the gray of dawn, Tay heard the dragon belching, caught a glimpse of the Huey whump-whump-whumping in stasis, ahead, above the trees, and suddenly burst from the undergrowth into a rainswept clearing. His nerves thrilled as he sensed that the kill was close.

The Huey was completely in sight now. It hovered, facing the opposite side of the clearing, thundering one hundred bullets a second at the perimeter. In a fiery roaring blur, the edge of the forest was torn apart.

And directly in front of him, at his feet, Tay saw two furrows where the American and his helper had rushed through the knee-high grass across the clearing. His men gathered anxiously behind him. Tay slowly, excitedly, moved forward. He saw no indication that his quarry had doubled back on the furrows they had made. The grass, every blade of it, lay in the same direction, toward where the Huey was devastating the forest. Even if his quarry had walked backward, returning in this direction, the pressed-down pattern of the grass would still have retained a subtle sign of it. No, they had gone straight ahead, and the anger of the dragon confirmed that they weren't far away.

Tay reached the middle of the clearing, and here the tracks had been totally obliterated by the dragon's wrath, but it didn't matter—the Huey was pointing the way.

But lest it kill him by mistake, Tay used his field radio to contact the cossack, to alert him that the ground team had arrived, and as the gun stopped belching, Tay passed below the rotor-wash and the whump-whump-whump of the Huey, stalked through the devastated edge of the forest, and reached the continuation of the prisoner's trail.

But the footprints in the mud were deeper—only one set of them.

Tay's heart skipped when he saw the blood. Fresh blood. Not yet diluted by the rain.

One of them had been hit, was being carried by the other, by the American the large deep bootprints suggested.

Enthralled by the narrowing chase, Tay hurried forward. His heart skipped a second time when he found the impression where the prisoner had fallen with his burden. More blood.

Much more.

And here! Farther on, he saw where the prisoner had begun to crawl, dragging his accomplice.

Soon. Tay felt disappointed. It would be too laughably easy.

— 24 —

Rambo knelt before Co's grave. He had lifted her body and almost in a trance carried it deeper into the forest.

Her frail arms had dangled pathetically. When he found a sheltered spot that he thought she would like, rimmed by rocks, clustered with the orchids of death that she had once talked about—yesterday morning, two hundred years ago— he'd used his knife and, when that became too slow, his hands to dig the hole. He'd known that he was taking a risk by using up precious time to bury her. He didn't care. She herself had been precious, and if he could help it, no scavenging animals would ravage her body.

He dug until he reached thickly meshed impassable roots and gently, with reverence, lowered her into it.

About to cover her, he obeyed an impulse, removed her golden Buddha good-luck medallion, and hung it around his neck.

He cut a strip of cloth from her dress and with great deliberation, as a priest would dress for a ritual, tied it securely—a sweatband—around his forehead.

He covered her. The wet earth sinking over her, he saved her face till last, imagining how even a dead face must feel to have mud sink over it. When her lovely features, too, were gone, he brought stones to the mound and pulled vines over them, disguising the burial site.

And once again kneeled, almost as if in prayer.

But with his bow and the quiver of arrows slung across his back, with the primeval muck of the forest clinging everywhere to him, his hair, his face, his chest, his arms, he felt less like a priest than a warrior.

From far back.

Long ago.

When all of this had begun.

And had never stopped.

As rain streaked past his eyes, blurring them, he realized that what really blurred them were tears. At the camp, when he'd been tortured, seared by his own knife, jolted with electricity, he had cried. But those tears had been reflexive, an unwilled response to pain.

These tears, though, were different.

Caused by grief.

An emotion he'd thought he was no longer capable of.

He rose to his feet. Clenched his fists.

Spread his muscular arms.

Raised his anguished face to the stormy sky.

And shrieked, his vocal cords straining, bulging like knotted strands of leather. The scream rose louder, fuller.

He couldn't stop.

His years of frustration released their total fury. The first time, he hadn't asked to come here. He'd been told to come. Because other people had their reasons, people who went to sleep at night between clean sheets, with their bellies full. It wasn't *my* war. But I fought it for them.

And became an embarrassment to them, because they knew there'd been too many lies, and the way to undo a lie is to pretend it never happened—so they made believe I'd never existed. And others called me baby-killer.

The second time, I didn't want to come here either. But they said they were willing to clean up the mess they'd made, to try to correct their mistakes. And *someone* had to get those prisoners back, because the people who slept between clean sheets sure as hell couldn't do it. So I fought their war a second time, and again they lied and did what they could to keep me from winning it and wanted to make believe I never existed.

Well, I'm through fighting other people's wars.

Yes, this time, I'll fight my own.

And *this* time, no one's going to stop me from winning.

Far away, he heard the whump-whump-whump of the Huey, but closer he heard men charging through the forest.

All right, he thought, squinting with hate—and grief as he stared at the grave. If you guys want a fight...

You got it.

The war had begun.

– 7 –

THE BLOOD ZONE

— I —

Soon now, Tay thought ecstatically, charging through the forest. The muddy footprints he followed were closer together—sure evidence of fatigue. And each toe made a streak in the mud, as if the American did not have the strength to lift his boots. Weakened to begin with, the American was no doubt ready to collapse from the burden he carried. The hunt would end in minutes.

Possibly seconds.

But I have to be cautious, Tay reminded himself. Even an exhausted animal can fight back briefly. There's no need to end this sport too quickly. It might be fun to prolong it slightly.

He held up his hand, signaling the soldiers behind him to stop. Fascinated, he turned to explain the need for caution and frowned when he counted one less man than he expected. Of course, on the bluff above the base, a soldier had tripped a boobytrap and been dismembered. But Tay had made allowance for that.

He ought to have ten men.

He had nine.

Another boobytrap? he wondered. Or perhaps a soldier had fallen and sprained an ankle. Or even got lost in the dark.

The man would show up. And when he did, Tay would let him know what it felt like to lose face.

Tay blinked. The rain played tricks on him, he was sure. The soldier nearest him abruptly had an object appear on his chest.

A stick.

An arrow.

Blood.

As the soldier fell back, another soldier had an arrow in his chest.

And Tay lunged, panicked, for cover, hearing screams around him.

A hiss. A third soldier fell, peering stupidly at an arrow in him.

Tay's men had already started firing. The combined stuttering blasts from their AK-47's stunned Tay's ears. As he shouted for them to stop, his voice seemed to come from far away. They fired blindly, shooting at everything before them—trees, bushes, vines, orchids—shredding leaves, splintering bark. Empty bullet casings flipped toward the mud.

And Tay—his equilibrium off-balanced by the strident ringing behind his ears—kept yelling for them to stop.

He shoved at them, cursing. They finally did what they were told. Crouched behind trees, they aimed trembling rifles, nervous, their eyes darting wildly.

And one more man had been killed, an arrow projecting grotesquely from his left eye, the shaft in far enough that the barb protruded from the back of his skull.

Tay wiped combined sweat and rain from his face. Glancing warily around, he tried to think.

And he didn't like his conclusions.

A minute ago, he'd had nine men. Now there were five. The bow from which these arrows came was powerful enough to kill on impact, the shock enormous. The vanes on the arrows were made from plastic, so the rain would not soften them and affect the accuracy of the archer's aim.

The *American's* aim?

But where would the American have found such a powerful bow, such well-designed arrows?

And now that the accumulated roar of the AK-47's had ruined everyone's hearing, the archer could sneak more easily through the forest without fear of snapping a branch or rustling leaves. If he doesn't show himself...

...we can't know where he is to shoot at him.

Tay hunched even lower and spoke to his handheld radio.

— 2 —

Maintaining the Huey's static position over the clearing, Yashin pressed his earphones closer to his head, shutting out the chopper's chugging roar.

He heard an unsteady voice. "Search One to Dragon. Search One to Dragon. Come in."

Yashin acknowledged.

"Dragon, we are under attack. Four dead."

Surprised, Yashin kept his voice flat. "Draw his fire. He'll soon run out of ammunition. Over."

"Dragon, repeat. I do not receive you."

Impatient, Yashin spoke louder. "Draw his fire!"

"Dragon, he's too well hidden."

"Shoot at his gunfire."

"Dragon, I do not receive you."

Yashin spoke even louder. "Have you got shit in your ears? Shoot at his gunfire!"

"Dragon, he isn't using a gun."

This time, Yashin did allow himself to sound surprised. "Not a gun? Then what...?"

"A bow and arrow."

Bow and...?

Yashin abruptly heard a commotion—someone screaming, other men shouting, AK-47's rattling. He bit his lower lip with his broken teeth as the shots kept on and on.

— 3 —

It had taken all night for the camp's incompetent electrician to get the generator working again, but now that the overhead light was on, it didn't matter. Despite the murky rain outside, the morning was bright enough for Podovsk to see the radio.

And communications mattered more than light. Very much. He'd stayed behind to coordinate the search, to receive transmissions from the various search groups, Soviet and Vietnamese, and relay information from one to the other, and of course to Yashin with the dragon in the Huey. He's listened with keener anticipation as a Vietnamese patrol seemed about to recapture the American. The patrol was commanded by Sergeant Tay, who'd earlier seemed as incompetent as the camp's electrician, deserving his assignment here, but as Tay's reports had become more affirmative, Podovsk had wondered if he'd misjudged the man. Results deserved a reward. If the sergeant brought back a trophy, Podovsk decided, he'd earn himself a transfer out of here.

But that had been fifteen minutes ago.

Now as Podovsk's enthusiasm drained sickly from him, the sergeant's chances for a transfer became almost non-existent. The change in the situation was startling. Depressing. Podovsk stared at the radio, almost unable to believe the transmission Yashin was relaying to him.

Two minutes ago, Tay had reported that his group was under attack. Four men killed.

By a bow and arrow? What was going on out there?

Then the radio had crackled with shooting.

And now Tay reported that three other men had been killed. Tay—his voice distorted by panic—and two remaining men were in retreat.

A bow and arrow?

Podovsk abruptly switched to another frequency. "Search Two, Search Two!" His own voice was not as steady as he preferred. "This is Huntmaster! Do you read me? Over."

He spoke in Russian, gratified when he heard static broken by Russian acknowledgment.

"Search Two, proceed at once to northeast sector! Contact Dragon! Quarry has been located! Repeat! Quarry located!"

"Huntmaster, roger! On our way!"

Though the Russian voice sounded loud, it wasn't from nervousness—not like that coward Tay. No, Podovsk's men always spoke that way. Brusque. Authoritative. Confident.

The pros from Dover.

Now that Tay had demonstrated that Podovsk's initial opinion of him had been valid, it was time to let professionals take charge.

And if the American was foolish enough to chase Tay and his few remaining men, that was all to the good. Podovsk's airborne squad would have to go less distance to intercept him. And the American would soon discover that a bow and arrow were not much use against a unit that knew what it was doing.

A sudden angry thought made him leave the barracks. Captain Vinh. For several hours now, Podovsk hadn't seen him. Vinh was in camp, though. Podovsk was sure of that. Vinh had insisted that he had to remain here, in charge of the soldiers who guarded the camp and its prisoners.

Well, that's what *he* thinks, Podovsk decided, furious, striding through rain and mud toward the neighboring barracks. Vinh can get his uniform dirty the same as his men do. The same as *my* men. The same as *me*.

As if unconsciously to prove his point, Podovsk slipped in the mud and fell to one knee. His pants clung, wet, filthy, to his leg when he stood. Vinh can get his ass out there and hunt for the prisoner the same as the others. He's not doing anything.

The thought brightened Podovsk's spirits. And a further thought brightened them even more. Of course, there's really no need for Vinh to go. My airborne unit will have executed the American in—Podovsk glanced at his military watch as he slogged through the mud—oh, let's say forty minutes. But Vinh deserves the exercise. He needs to make an effort for a change.

All the same, as Podovsk neared the barracks, he suddenly wondered if he ought to go back to the radio.

But not to listen with satisfaction to the reports of the narrowing hunt.

Instead . . . as an extra precaution . . . there's really no need . . . but just in case.

To make sure.

Yes, he wondered. Perhaps he ought to radio for reinforcements.

Because if the American could turn back his hunters with nothing more than a bow and arrow, what might he be able to do if he got his hands on a decent weapon?

And Podovsk's spirits dimmed.

— 4 —

"Sir, AWACS is picking up some awfully strange reports," the radio technician said.

Trautman, under military guard, stood angrily at the side

of the hangar, watching Murdock's people continue packing up.

The "sir," of course, was directed not at Trautman but at Murdock, who pivoted sweating toward the technician. "Strange reports?"

"From Rambo's last position. When he called in."

As if Murdock didn't want to be reminded of Rambo's threat—*"Murdock, I'm coming for you."*—he barked at a workman going by who nearly dropped a crate, "Be careful! That decoder's worth two years of your pay!"

As the workman blanched, Murdock swung again to the radio technician. "So what's so strange?"

"Well, it seems there's..."

"Say it, for Christ's sake!"

"Some kind of battle going on. I don't know. The way the Communists are talking, it might as well be a war."

"... War?" Frowning, Murdock stalked closer.

Trautman felt a spark of excitement in his chest.

"With Rambo," the technician said.

"What?"

The spark of excitement in Trautman's chest glowed warmer.

"The way I'm getting it," the technician said, "and it's hard to know for sure—the transmissions keep overlapping—Rambo was being held a prisoner when he called us." The technician tried to listen to his earphones and talk to Murdock at once. "But he got away and..."

"Dammit! What?"

"Well, he killed seven, maybe eight, soldiers with the bow and arrow. After that, he stabbed a Russian. He strangled a Vietnamese with a vine. He strangled another Vietnamese with the string on his bow. He impaled a Russian with a spear. He's picking up their AK-47's and shooting till they're empty. He's even rigged some kind of catapult and brained a Russian with a rock."

"Spears and slingshots," Trautman said from the corner. "Isn't that what you said he was good at?"

"Just shut the fuck up!" Murdock snapped.

"And here's the weirdest part," the technician said. "This drove the Communists out of their minds."

"You're going to make me ask?" Murdock shouted.

"He got his hands on a Soviet, threw the guy from a bush, and the other Commies thought the Russian was Rambo and shot him to pieces."

"That's something I didn't tell you," Trautman said.

"What's that?" Murdock glared.

"The kid's adaptable."

"And now the Soviet who's taken charge of the base," the technician said, ". . . wait a second, I'm getting something." He nodded. "Yeah, the Soviet sent for reinforcements. He's called in help from all the Vietnamese soldiers at nearby bases. He's asked for a crack Soviet platoon from his own base at Cam Ranh Bay. And . . . yeah, he's got a . . . holy shit . . . a Soviet MIL MI-24 flying in. Christ, a chopper that big, with that kind of fire power, cannons, rockets, heat-seaking missiles, you'd think they were fighting Nam all over again."

"Well, in a way"—Trautman straightened—"they are."

Murdock spun. "Make sense!"

"The same as that police chief back in the States had the war brought home to him."

"I said make sense!"

"That town. The police chief figured he had the cops from towns all over the state. He had the State Police. The National Guard. Not to mention every asshole civilian with a rifle who thought he was Daniel Boone. So how could all of them lose? Well"—Trautman's voice was steel-sharp— "they found out. Because they didn't understand what *elite* meant. They never grasped what men like Rambo were taught to do. What Rambo *is*. That's why we call it *Special* Forces. But he came back and showed them, didn't he? Gave them a practical demonstration. Helped with their urban renewal project. No extra charge. Made a few renovations. What he actually did was, Murdock—in case you didn't read his file as closely as you claim—he leveled the whole damned town for them."

"All right." Murdock bristled. "Don't make me lose my patience. Just what the hell's your point?"

"Point? Simple. That Soviet commander's about to get a taste of what that cop felt. A practical demonstration all his own. He's going to learn how this is done."

"You've got an awful lot of misplaced confidence in your so-called—"

"Confidence? I ought to have. I trained him, after all. And when he's finished in Nam..."

"*If*, Colonel."

"*When* he's finished over there, remember what I told you. He always finishes what he starts. That cop found out. So will that Soviet commander... And so will you. When he's through kicking ass over there, he'll do what he promised. He'll come for you."

— 5 —

Breathing hard, trailing vines, camouflaged by branches tied to his back and arms, Rambo burst from the dense tangled forest as if a chunk of it had assumed human shape. Squawking chickens flapped off in all directions. Surprised, he faced the muddy dooryard of a hootch, one of twelve in this small village. Pigs scattered, grunting, as he sprinted across the yard, leaped over a low rail fence, and darted between two huts. Behind him, louder than the chickens and pigs, he heard the angry shouts of soldiers, both Soviet and Vietnamese, as they broke hurriedly through the underbrush.

From the hootches, he veered left down a muddy narrow lane, pushing through villagers, clearing a swath. The peasants didn't need encouragement. They bolted terrified toward huts, shouting in panic. Their reaction was understandable. Bad enough the sudden unexplained arrival of a fierce American. Worse, he was a giant by their standards. And worst of all, he looked like a mud-caked nightmare, vines and brambles on him, his face a mask of dark bloody earth topped by filth-encrusted hair.

He crashed against a gaping young man on a bicycle, spilling them both in a clatter of spokes. In a roll, he came up running. Ahead, he saw a battered truck jouncing out of the village, its backfires like gunshots, and changing his course, he raced to intercept it. The truck, rusted and mud-caked into a brownish lump on wheels, hauled a load of chickens in wire mesh cages in back. He reached the cab, leaped onto the running board, and as the startled old man at the wheel reflexively took his foot off the accelerator, Rambo pointed his knife and shouted in Vietnamese, "Keep driving!"

The old man obeyed, increasing speed again. Rambo clung to the door as the truck bounced and rattled along the rutted road. On his left, a line of trees ended. The road now cut through a field of tall thick elephant grass. To the right, he saw soldiers charge from the forest. Behind him, other soldiers raced down the road from the village. And this time, what he thought were backfires were gunshots. A bullet shattered the filthy back window, chickens squawking in terror. From ahead, a bullet burst the muddy windshield. As glass flew into the cab, the old man at the wheel flung his hands to his face. The truck veered out of control, sped toward a ditch, and slued abruptly down, jolting, water flying as the truck flopped onto its side.

Rambo tumbled clear, hearing the old man sob helplessly. I'm sorry, Rambo thought as chickens scattered from their broken cages. I didn't have a choice. At least you weren't hurt. He grabbed a rusted gas can from the twisted wreckage in the truck's bed and sprinted toward the thick tall grass, at once disappearing.

— 6 —

But he'll leave a trail, Tay thought, overcome with fury. A stupidly obvious trail through the grass, and this time he'll need more than a bow and arrow against *all* of us.

As Tay ran up to the overturned truck, pausing to catch his breath, he felt encouraged by the many soldiers who joined him.

All of us, indeed. Podovsk's urgently radioed orders had resulted in a massive buildup of personnel. Units from everywhere around had rushed here to join the hunt. The more men the American killed, the more the soldiers were determined to pay him back. Two hundred. More on the way. And that didn't count the MIL helicopter, the massive flying arsenal, that Podovsk had sent for.

Tay's chest expanded as he anticipated, deliciously, his revenge.

Two troop trucks roared along the road, skidding to a stop, throwing mud. Captain Vinh jumped down from one cab as soldiers tumbled from the back. Tay hid his amusement at the muck that splashed onto Vinh's usually immaculate uniform. Thinks he's such a gentleman. Figures he's above it all. Well, Podovsk kicked his ass for him, and now he's down here with the rest of us. We'll see how he likes it.

Ignoring the stains on his uniform, Vinh strode with exaggerated military bearing toward his men. He glared at the eight-foot-tall grass. He pointed down at the trampled stalks where the American had disappeared into the grass. There was blood on the path.

Tay swallowed his anger, feeling Vinh slap his shoulder.

"There!" Vinh said. "You see? Now we find where he's crawled to die!"

Tay thought: Sure, you're great at giving orders, but what you really mean is *I'll* have to find where he's crawled.

Not that Tay minded. He was anxious to pay the American back for his accumulating insults. He stepped ahead and gestured toward soldiers to follow him.

But Vinh surprised him, slapping his shoulder again. "Not you! You've had your chance! Now I'll guarantee that the job is done correctly!"

Pushing past Tay, Vinh stepped down into the watery ditch, shuddered as he waded through it, and stood at the entrance to the path through the towering grass. The soldiers scrambled to join him, splashing across the ditch, and even before they reached the top, Vinh had already entered the grass. They hurried after him, disappearing. Only the tips of the radio antennas showed above the waving stalks. Then the antennas, too, were gone.

Tay bitterly stared at the field. Sure, when it comes to an obvious trail, Vinh figures he's an expert tracker. He gets to do the easy part.

And take all the credit.

And get transferred.

Shit.

— 7 —

Fifty nerve-wracking paces into the grass, knowing he could not be seen from the road, Vinh began to lag back, letting other soldiers move ahead of him.

"Look sharply! Watch out for tricks!"

Hanging farther back, he glanced uneasily around him. The grass, pressing close against him on each side, made him feel smothered. The air in here was much more humid and heavy than back at the road. And the sounds were eerie—the swish of the grass, the echo of voices from the road, the overhead cry of a bird that turned in a spiral, staring down at him. He wondered if there'd be snakes in here.

The only thing that reassured him was the wide trail of blood that the American, obviously wounded badly, had left behind.

Sweat dripped off Vinh's face. The underarms of his captain's jacket were soaked. He wondered if it would be unmilitary to roll up his sleeves.

Fate, he decided, had not been kind. True, he'd managed to avoid combat during the war, his plush assignment in Hanoi marred occasionally by capitalist bombing, though the bombs had never fallen close to his office or his apartment in the city. With subordinates to perform his duties, he'd spent many lovely days on his sampan with his mistress. On his mistress, too. The thought made him smile despite his present circumstances. But one day his superior officer had been replaced, and the next thing Vinh had known, he'd been sent to the outposts. That thought made him frown again. At once, yet another thought brightened him, almost exactly as the clouds opened and the sun blazed down.

Yes, but if I can catch the American, I'll be a hero of the republic.

I'll soon be back in Hanoi.

Puzzled voices ahead of him made him pay attention to what he was doing here. The column of men stopped. Vinh pushed past them.

"Well, what's the problem?" he asked indignantly. "Keep searching! Find him!"

As he reached the front, passing them all, he noticed the lead soldier's uncomprehending expression and then frowned down at its cause.

Blood.

Two chickens, their heads cut off, lay against a can.

The cap of the can was on the ground between the chicken heads.

It seemed some kind of shrine. No doubt, the remnants of some bizarre religious ritual.

These villagers, he thought with contempt. The primitive notions they get.

Then sniffing the air, he realized that the can had been used for carrying gas.

He smelled something else. What was it?

Smoke?

The flames shot through the grass on his right, whooshing, snaking toward him through the waving stalks.

"Get back!" Vinh's command wasn't motivated by concern for his men. He didn't mean, *Get away before you get hurt*. What he meant was, *You stupid idiots, get out of my way, clear the path!*

He pushed his men away, feeling sudden heat behind him.

But his men had the same idea. Falling over each other, shoving, they blocked the trail.

"Get back!"

The flames reached the can.

"Get . . . !"

Voom!

— **8** —

The blast resembled a mushroom cloud, though the cloud was actually flames. A solid rising ball of them. And its roar sent a visible shock wave rippling through the grass.

It made Tay stumble back. On the road at the edge of the field, he blinked in stupefaction. One second, the field had looked so boring, so peaceful, the sun blazing down on it, that Tay had yawned. The next second, a river of fire had streaked through the grass from the right. And a second after that, the center of the field had exploded.

He heard screams. Gunshots. Black smoke billowed from the field. The flames spread from the middle, sweeping through the grass toward the perimeter.

A man raced out of the grass. Shrieking, he was totally on fire, flailing his arms, swatting his chest. He staggered, fell to his knees, walked on them, and toppled into the ditch. Water hissed. The rising steam stank acridly of burned hair and scorched flesh.

But though the body was face down in the water, though the man's features had been consumed, unrecognizable, when he lunged from the grass, Tay knew who he was. Part of the insignia on his uniform had not been obliterated.

Captain Vinh.

The mutilated flesh was so obscene that Tay gaped in horror. He nonetheless had two distracting thoughts.

So you wanted to do the easy part and get all the glory, huh?

And second . . .

Your uniform's dirty.

— 9 —

Rambo crouched on the wooden bluff beyond the burning field. Past the rising black smoke, on the far side of the field, he saw the mass of soldiers react to the explosion and flames. Some rushed to help their comrades. Others stumbled back. He heard a whump-whump-whump that grew louder, and turning, he squinted with hate toward the Huey as it streaked above the village, approaching the field. Whoever was flying it had killed Co.

His grip tightened so hard on his bow that his knuckles ached.

And the pilot, he promised himself, would pay.

But first . . .

His arrows had another feature. Besides their all-black color, their plastic vanes, their strong yet lightweight aluminum shafts, and their wide four-bladed serrated Copperhead Ripper tips, they were hollow.

He unscrewed the middle of a shaft. From his quiver, he removed a container of C-4 plastic explosive, molded some of it into the shape of a worm, and dropped the worm down the hollow center of the shaft toward the tip. He reassembled the arrow and went through the same process with three others.

Next he unscrewed the Copperhead Ripper from each

shaft and replaced each with a lookalike broadhead.

The lookalike had one important difference. It was a detonator. On impact, its small explosive charge would set off the plastic explosive.

He set an arrow onto the bow, drew the string back to its full thirty-inch extension, and felt the wheels at the end of each bow limb roll over to adjust the pressure, reducing his effort from one hundred pounds to fifty as he aimed at one of the trucks on the road beyond the field. He shut out the world, except for the arrow, the bow, and the target. The universe stopped.

And began again as he released the arrow. The wheels on each limb compounded the thrust of the string, increasing its force from fifty pounds to one hundred. At the instant the arrow left the bow, it hissed at two hundred and fifty feet per second.

But he wasn't surprised that, because of the distance and the obscuring smoke, he missed the truck two hundred yards away. What he hit was sufficient, though. A section of road exploded. Men flew. Even from that far away, he heard screams in the midst of the blast.

He hurriedly corrected his aim, releasing another arrow. And this time he hit his mark, the truck erupting in a fiery wallop that was followed by a second explosion, the *va-room!* of the gas tank. Shrapnel and flames enveloped more soldiers.

He shot yet again.

The other truck disintegrated in a blazing roar.

And he even tried a shot at the Huey, but the arrow arced past it, descending, exploding near more soldiers on the road.

Enough.

He had to save his arrows. Earlier, after he'd routed Sergeant Tay's men in the forest, killing eight of them with arrows, he'd crept to each body. Though the tilted barbs on the Copperhead Ripper tip would normally not allow the shaft to be pulled back through the body, he could in this case easily retrieve the shaft by unscrewing the broadhead that protruded from the body and thus, with nothing to impede the shaft, pull the arrow out. He had then screwed the broadhead back onto each arrow.

But even then his supply was limited. He had to use them judiciously. As rifle fire was directed toward this bluff, the bullets not coming close to him, he eased back, deciding his next tactic.

But paused as he saw ten soldiers rush down the road and veer around the flaming grass, heading in this direction.

And the man who led them—it was hard to tell this far away—the man who led them . . .

. . . seemed to be Sergeant Tay.

As Rambo ducked down the brush-covered back of the slope, he heard the whump-whump-whump of the Huey.

— 10 —

"What is it now? Have they killed him yet?" Murdock demanded.

Flanked by guards, Trautman waited for the radio technician's answer.

The operator shook his head. "Sure doesn't sound like it."

"What the hell is *that* supposed to mean?" Murdock's face was an angry red.

"He just started a forest fire. He killed the Vietnamese officer in charge. He blew up two personnel trucks. And . . . No, this can't be right."

"Just tell me!"

"They're saying his body count is up to a hundred and ten."

Murdock's lips moved, no sound coming out. Slowly he turned toward the open bay of the hangar, staring toward the wooded hills.

Northeast, Trautman knew. Toward...

"What in God's name is going on over there?" Murdock asked.

— II —

Tay shifted through the forest. Mosquitoes feasted on his sweaty face, but he didn't dare distract himself by swatting at their itchy cluster.

His men were arranged in a spread-out phalanx formation, those at the sides and the rear facing outward or backward as they crept warily through the steamy clinging underbrush. Every sound made them flinch.

Tay told himself, he can't have many arrows left. All we have to do is keep tracking him, keep wearing his strength down. After what Podovsk and Yashin did to him at the camp, after the distance he's run, the fight he's put up, he has to be getting weak.

But Tay was much less confident than he'd been at the start of the hunt. Indeed, he wondered why he'd been so foolish as to lead these soldiers up here. The excitement of the moment, perhaps. The need to avenge his comrades. The hope of earning a transfer.

Yes, he decided. All of those.

But were they enough to offset his fear? He'd assumed that many more men would follow him. The small group that actually had come along made him now feel exposed, even naked.

But the factor that tilted the balance, that made him keep tracking, searching, was far too strong to be ignored.

The simple truth was that, already consumed by hate because of his first humiliation when the American had escaped from him years before, he was now even more enraged because of his second humiliation when earlier today the American's arrows had made him flee in face-losing panic.

Other soldiers had laughed at him.

And for that, the American would have his privates cut off and stuck in his mouth.

The arrow struck the soldier ahead of him in the mouth, ramming past his teeth, protruding from the back of his skull. The death was so grotesque that the other soldiers broke from the phalanx, lunging for cover, shooting everywhere, at nothing.

And no! It was happening all over again, just like this morning, the need to panic growing in him. And this time— *no!*—he wouldn't allow it.

Shouting at his men, insulting them, shoving, kicking, his heart thundering, he forced them toward the direction of the archer.

And suddenly one of them fell out of sight, enveloped by a sinkhole that the American had disguised. When Tay peered down, he saw stakes in the man, in his neck, his chest, his privates.

The soldiers stumbled back.

"Keep moving!" Tay screamed, his stomach on fire. "Or I'll shoot you myself!"

A spear struck another man.

And Tay almost shrieked in triumph. "He's out of arrows! Keep going after him! He'll soon be just throwing rocks!"

The stutter of the AK-47 made him livid. From a soldier behind him.

Tay turned in fury. "Not yet, you idiot! Don't waste your ammunition! Don't shoot till you see him!"

Though Tay kept screaming, he already saw that the AK-47 was not being fired by one of his men. It came from farther back, from the undergrowth. The American had picked up a dead man's rifle!

Tay's men fell, riddled by 7.62-mm bullets.

Diving behind a fallen tree, Tay caught a glimpse of his quarry. The American, camouflaged with vines, leaves, and brambles clinging to him, encrusted with mud, looked like a demon sprung from the earth. He crouched with the rifle aimed at Tay. Their angry gazes met.

And the AK-47 stopped firing. The American stared down at the rifle, threw it away, and ran.

But not in Tay's direction.

In retreat!

Ecstatic, Tay stumbled up from behind the fallen tree. He raised his rifle and began to fire, shredding leaves. He emptied the magazine and grabbed another AK-47 from the ground, stalking forward shooting.

He started to laugh.

You used all your arrows. You camouflaged a pungi pit. You threw a spear.

You even got your hands on a rifle, but now it's out of bullets, and all you've got is your knife.

Well, I've got *lots* of bullets, and after I empty a magazine into your chest, I'm going to use that knife to cut off your . . .

Tay stopped, amazed. He lost his balance, lurched back, but concentrated and regained his footing.

He felt very puzzled.

I was sure, he thought.

I was sure you'd used all your arrows.

But he understood how wrong he'd been.

Because one of them now projected from his stomach. A magic act of now-you-don't-see-it and now-you-do.

And more important, now you feel it.

Yes. Oh, my, yes.

And it hurt so much. Like several razors slicing into him.

With a force that took his breath away.

This happened in one second.

And in the next—he had an infinitesimal part of that second to realize awesomely—his guts blew apart.

— 12 —

For the scars on my back and chest, Rambo thought. And the scars in my mind. And the nightmares that never stopped.

But he still had another scar, deeper, more agonizing—the death of Co.

He heard the whump-whump-whump of the Huey rushing over the forest. That's it. Come closer, he thought. Come closer. In rage, he retrieved an arrow from one of the soldiers he'd shot. As before, he would fill the shaft with plastic explosive and attach a detonator head.

If he could lure the Huey close to him, trick the pilot into hovering away from trees so there'd be nothing to deflect the arrow, he could bring down the son-of-a-bitch. Bring him down? Hell, blow him into specks.

But he had to be careful. The Huey had a dragon.

As he worked to retrieve an arrow from a body, the helicopter suddenly showed itself beyond a gap in the trees. Peering up, startled, Rambo clearly saw the face of the pilot beyond the Plexiglas.

The cossack.

And the cossack straightened, seeing him.

No time for the arrow.

Sprinting, planning to double back and get it once he had the chance, Rambo veered past trees, slashing madly through bushes. He felt his shoulder blades tense. Any moment, the dragon would belch. The thunderous fiery column of bullets would follow the path he made through the forest, disintegrating his cover, isolating him until...

But his cover began to disappear on its own, receding, dwindling. Shadows diminished. Sunlight grew.

My God, another clearing.

Can't let him catch me in the open.

Veering to the left, Rambo raced through scattered trees. But he didn't understand. The dragon had stopped. He's got a chance for me, but he isn't' taking it. Out of ammunition?

He risked a frantic glance up behind him. The Huey continued its roaring approach. But the dragon still didn't belch, and he was even more sure that the gun was empty. In its place, he heard the stuttering blast of a smaller gun, an M-60.

And saw two objects flip from the Huey's open bay. Two long metal cylinders. Instead of falling straight down, they were carried forward by the speed they'd gained from the Huey, slanting in his direction, beginning to tumble.

Worse than the dragon.

Napalm!

Rambo raced, desperate, his lungs swelling, aching, his legs pumping, stretching for maximum distance.

Ahead, through the undergrowth, he saw something glint from right to left. And behind, he heard the wallop of the canisters rupturing onto the ground, a powerful liquid-exploding *va-room!* that grew and streaked and chased him. Twenty-meter-long arcs of flame would be spewing through the forest. He smelled sick-sweet fumes, felt heat on his back, even saw his shadow ahead of him, though the sun blazed overhead.

And as the flames began to sear his back, their massive rush throwing him forward, he dove, adding to the momentum of their push.

Toward the glint he'd seen through the trees.

A rushing stream. Plunging into it, he felt the water cool his stinging back. He slanted lower into the water, kicking, thrusting with his arms. As the rushing current twisted him, he saw the surface, the flames sweeping over the water. The current twisted him again, and facing the bottom, he saw that the blazing napalm made the stream's muddy bottom look orange.

Propelled, he scraped past boulders, wincing, trying to hold his breath. The stream dipped, rose, and dipped again, a grotesque amusement park ride gone insane, and as the flames above him disappeared, unable to hold his breath anymore, he struggled toward the surface, clawing through the water.

The stream disappeared. His stomach rose as his body dropped. In sunlight, his lungs expanding, inhaling as he plummeted, he heard a rumble below him. The rumble amplified as he fell. A cataract. And all at once, the rumble was directly against his ears, his body plunging into the pool at the bottom. Stunned by the splashing shock, he swallowed water, gagged, and kicked against a boulder he'd barely missed. He surfaced, gasping, spun by turbulence.

Rubbing his eyes to clear them, he strained, peering up. High, on the escarpment, a firestorm raged.

And swooping past it, the Huey resumed its attack.

Bullets from the roaring M-60 splintered the rocky shore behind him.

And the dragon? Out of bullets?

No! It belched.

And Rambo, inhaling frantically, dove kicking clawing toward the pressure at the bottom of the seething pool.

— 13 —

Yashin watched the pool enlarge beyond the Huey's Plexiglas as the chopper rushed down the chasm. He licked his broken teeth, feeling their jagged edges, like broken glass, on his tongue. With his thumb hard on the dragon's firing button, he watched the fusillade churn the pool, making the water seem to boil. In the bay behind him, a gunner strafed the pool with M-60 rounds. Yashin wanted to empty his service pistol at it. To throw empty ammunition cases at it. To piss on it.

He took his thumb off the dragon's firing button. The gunner behind him stopped the M-60. The churning pool returned to its normal frothing turbulence. Yashin urged the Huey closer to it.

"Do you see his body?" he shouted to the two soldiers in back.

They stared out the open ports on each side but didn't answer.

"The swirl of water should bring it to the surface!"

Or maybe not, Yashin thought. If there's an undercurrent, his body might have been caught between rocks at the bottom.

"Then what about blood?" he shouted. "Do you see any blood?"

They didn't, and neither did he.

But the American *couldn't* have survived!

Unless the turbulence dissipated the blood so much that

it wasn't obvious. He lowered the Huey. He had to look closer.

"You!" he shouted to one of the soldiers, the man who normally flew this helicopter. "Take the controls! I'm going back there!"

The soldier obeyed, and Yashin stalked toward the back, peering out the open bay on the left, staring down.

No blood.

"Take it lower!" he told the pilot.

"But we're almost into the water now."

"Take it lower!"

The pilot obeyed.

The water churned directly below him as Yashin studied its concealing froth. Mist from the rumbling waterfall entered the chopper.

This is pointless, Yashin thought. We'll get ourselves killed.

And then he realized, the current would have carried the body downstream. That's why I don't see blood. The blood will show up farther along.

He nodded and told the pilot, "Take it up. Follow the stream!"

The pilot looked relieved to do so. As the Huey slowly rose, the soldier next to Yashin exhaled.

And suddenly clutched the bulkhead, fighting to keep his balance as the Huey tilted.

Yashin yelled to the pilot, "What's the matter with you?"

"Air currents! From the waterfall!"

The Huey tilted again.

"Keep it steady!"

"I'm trying! The wind is—!"

Disgusted, Yashin glanced toward the soldier clutching the bulkhead across from him.

But the soldier wasn't there.

Yashin glimpsed the blur of his uniform as he fell out of sight toward the water.

And the American was surging up into the bay, dripping, filthy, his eyes like lasers.

He'd been hanging onto one of the landing skids, Yashin realized. That was why the Huey had tilted. Because its weight wasn't balanced. He must have lunged from the water as the chopper started to rise.

These frantic thoughts occurred to him as he drew his pistol.

But the American surged across the compartment, grabbing his wrist, preventing him from aiming. Yashin dug his fingers into the American's face, trying to jab out those burning eyes. Locked in a grotesque dance, they staggered back and forth, sideways, listing toward one open bay, then the other.

Blocking a blow to his larynx, Yashin kicked at his enemy's crotch. But the American dodged and struck Yashin's gun arm, his wrist, the blow so powerful that Yashin's fingers opened reflexively, the pistol clattering onto the metal floor, sliding out the bay.

Like wrestlers, they crouched, circling each other.

The Huey tilted again. But this time Yashin knew exactly why. The pilot was trying to make the American lose his balance.

If I don't lose mine first.

They struck at each other, crashing against the wall by the dragon's ammunition canister. The Huey yawed and recovered. Open space roared outside as Yashin aimed a blow toward the bridge of his enemy's nose. The Huey pitched again.

The next thing Yashin knew, as his heart pounded wildly, he'd stumbled backward half out the door. He grabbed its side, suspended horribly, hanging above a rushing blur of forest. Wind tugged his uniform. And with an angry scream, he surged back into the helicopter.

This time, the Huey pitched in the other direction. The American tumbled back as Yashin struck his chest.

And the American went out the door.

— 14 —

Rambo grabbed at the first thing he saw as he left the bay. The M-60 doorgun on its mount. He snagged its handles as he went past. The gun swung with him. The bolts that held the mount to the floor took a terrible strain as he dangled, leaves rushing past his boots.

The Soviet screamed in triumph, stalking forward.

Releasing one hand from the grips at the back of the gun, raising that hand, Rambo pulled the M-60's bolt back, arming it. The barrel pointed inside the chopper.

And shuddering as he dangled, he pulled the trigger, firing a point-blank burst at the cossack. The roar seemed louder than the rotors and the windstream. As empty casings glinted through the air, bullets shattered the Russian's chest, jerking him back through the other door. He saw an explosive spray of blood.

For Co, he thought.

For Co.

And the Russian was gone.

But Rambo felt a lurch as the Huey descended closer to the treetops, pitching, dipping, the pilot obviously trying to sweep him off. With both hands on the M-60 now, Rambo pulled himself higher. Straining, sweating, he grabbed the side of the door and scrambled in.

He angrily drew his knife.

He surged toward the pilot...

...who flinched as the knife touched his neck.

"I'll give you a choice."

The pilot took the second option. Avoiding the knife, he squirmed from his seat, backing toward the open door.

And fell out, screaming as the Huey pitched again and Rambo grabbed the controls.

— 15 —

"That's it. Except for the generator, everything else is loaded," Murdock said. "We need the radio."

The hangar was a massive echoing shell. Outside its gloom, the Peregrine jet and Agusta chopper waited in sunlight, crammed full, ready for takeoff. Other choppers had landed to transport the other equipment. Men stood, ready to board.

But the radio technician pressed his earphones closer to his head and held up a hand as if he didn't want to miss something.

"I said dismantle the radio," Murdock ordered.

Trautman, still under guard, came to attention when he saw the fascinated look on the radio technician's face.

"I think you'll want to hear this," the technician said.

"Ah . . ." Murdock relaxed. "He's dead."

"Not quite, sir. I'm getting frantic messages from the Soviet officer at the camp. He can't get the Soviet pilot in the chopper to respond. For a while, he thought the chopper might have crashed."

"For a while?" Murdock frowned. "Then something else happened to it?"

"Well, yes, sir. The Soviet officer's pretty sure now it was commandeered."

"Say that again."

"Rambo. It seems he, uh, took it."

"What?"

"He . . . took it."

"Christ almighty! That can't be true."

"Well, the reason the Soviet thinks so . . . the reason he's making frantic calls for help . . ."

Trautman wanted to grin.

". . . the chopper's attacking the camp. Fact is, it's blowing it to hell."

Murdock stared as if with utter incomprehension.

"I told you," Trautman said. "The kid's adaptable."

Murdock sighed and slowly swung toward the loaded Peregrine and Agusta, the other choppers packed with equipment, the men getting ready to board.

He shouted, his voice startlingly amplified by the cavernous hangar, "Everybody! I want that stuff unpacked! Get it all back in here!"

"What?" An aide walked mystified to the hangar's entrance.

Ericson and Doyle stood suddenly next to the man.

"Get it all back in here!" Murdock seemed to swell. "This fucking mission isn't over yet!"

— 16 —

The heat haze cleared, and through the Huey's Plexiglas, Rambo saw the camp. He pressed his thumb on the dragon's firing button. A flash descended. The guard tower on the left disintegrated, becoming a cloud of falling splinters. The dragon's thunder rolled across the valley.

He pivoted the Huey. The dragon roared again. Orange lightning vaporized the tower on the right. And even more furious, he kept pivoting, pressing the trigger. Guards raised their rifles, aiming, bursting apart like balloons gorged with blood. The barracks on the right no longer existed. The one in the middle—where he'd been tortured—erupted into specks of flaming wreckage. He vaporized the sentry post at the gate. Three soldiers who ran behind a truck were atomized when the truck exploded, ripped open like aluminum foil, shrapnel flying. Red haze and tattered uniforms floated through the air.

Yes!

He wanted to scream it. Yes!

Or maybe he did scream. Maybe the hideous shriek he thought he heard from down there was actually from his own strained, stretched, raw vocal cords, his angry twisted mouth. He'd never know.

He flattened, annihilated, *obliterated* the barracks on the left, where he himself had been held.

Yes!

And he kept shooting, couldn't stop himself, the dragon roaring, razing another guard post, blowing apart another truck. *Everything!*

The nightmares might end if he sent it all to hell!

If he made it no longer exist.

But nothing existed. Wasn't that what his tribesman teacher had taught him?

The way of Zen?

Then why did it feel so good to destroy what didn't exist?

Because you're imperfect.

No. Because I've had it, man. I got pushed in that town. And these bastards pushed me here. And Murdock abandoned me. And Co got killed.

And now I'm *pissed!*

He settled the Huey onto the ground. He shut off the engine, charged toward the rear, and detached the M-60 from its mount. Clutching it, ignoring the terrible weight, its ammunition belt slung over his back, he stalked from the Huey angrily through the heat haze and smoke. Encrusted with mud, vines, branches, brambles, blood, sweat, feeling his eyes blaze like an angry burst from the dragon, he aimed the M-60 from his waist and shot at everything that wore a uniform.

He killed . . .

. . . and killed . . .

And killed.

And finally it was over.

— 17 —

Except for the crackle of flames, the camp was deathly silent.

Striding exhausted through the smoke and the wreckage, aiming the heavy, shoulder-aching, back-straining M-60 this way and that before him, he approached the cave behind the camp.

A soldier skittered terrified from behind a heap of rubble, racing in panic, weaponless, toward the forest. Rambo ignored him.

Another soldier shot at him from behind a tree. Rambo ricocheted bullets off a boulder next to the tree and sent him arcing into bushes.

And now through the smoke, he saw the bamboo bars that held the prisoners in the cave.

And the Soviet officer, Podovsk, standing in front of the bars, aiming his pistol toward the prisoners.

226

"We have what I believe is called a standoff," Podovsk said in English. His words suggested confidence, but his face was drained of all color.

And his voice shook.

Rambo kept coming.

"If you shoot me, my finger will jerk on the trigger, and one of these men will die."

Rambo came nearer.

"You didn't do all this so one of them would die at the moment of rescue."

"Take the chance and shoot the son-of-a-bitch," Banks growled behind the bars.

Rambo felt glad to hear his voice. He'd been afraid that Banks had been killed as a punishment for Rambo's escape.

"All I ask is your word that you'll let me go," Podovsk said. "My life for one of theirs."

But Rambo kept coming, and Podovsk shuddered.

"You won!" the Soviet shouted. "Isn't that enough?"

He turned abruptly to shoot Rambo, and a hand lunged between the bars, clutching Podovsk's wrist. The hand had almost no flesh. It might have belonged to a corpse come back from the grave to seek revenge. The bony grip should have had no strength, but it clung to Podovsk as if in a death grip. By the time the Soviet had twisted free, Rambo's own hand was on the Russian's wrist, twisting, snapping it like a piece of kindling.

Podovsk screamed. His pistol dropped.

And Rambo let the M-60 drop. It clattered. He grabbed the Soviet, dragged him struggling thirty yards across the compound—"No!"—lifted him by a leg and an arm.

High above Rambo's head.

"No!"

And threw him into the slime pit. Podovsk's scream died with a muddy splash.

Things covered him.

— 18 —

Technicians, helped by soldiers, hurried to reassemble equipment. The hangar was once again filled with frantic activity.

"Never mind that other stuff!" Murdock ordered. "I want the radar working first!"

Trautman shook his head, amazed, unable to adjust to the change in the man. After having abandoned Rambo and indeed been anxious for Rambo to die, Murdock was now working desperately to save him, to bring him back.

"Make sure the Agusta's empty!" Murdock ordered. "Ericson! Doyle! Double-check its weapons!"

For a stomach-sinking second, Trautman had a sudden premonition. There could be another reason for Murdock's behavior. Another motive entirely. Not to save Rambo. Not to bring him in. But . . .

No, surely not. Not even Murdock would . . .

— 19 —

Rambo aimed the M-60 on an angle away from the prisoners and shot off the lock on the bars that blocked the cave. He grabbed the gate and yanked it open. The prisoners stared, too stunned to talk or move.

But all at once, their awe became urgency.

"For Christ's sake, let's go!" Banks yelled.

The ones who still had strength lifted the sicker men to their feet. Rambo helped the man with malaria from the cave. They tried to hurry across the compound, but their progress was pathetic, like zombies, shuffling more than running. One man staggered. Banks grabbed him as he fell.

And at last they reached the Huey, but even then it wasn't over. A wounded soldier fired from the wreckage of a barracks, hitting a prisoner in the side, and Banks went crazy, grabbing an AK-47 off the ground, shooting until the soldier was riddled with bullet holes.

Banks looked so wild that Rambo understood—for this man, too, the nightmares wouldn't ever be over.

Or for the other men.

Until you died, nothing about this damned war ever left you.

Climbing, crawling, squirming into the Huey, they huddled together. Rambo lifted in the wounded man, hurried to reattach the M-60 on its mount, and rushed toward the chopper's controls. As the rotors began to turn and the engine whined increasingly, he heard another sound, faint, hardly audible.

But he heard it all the same. And looking back, he saw what caused it. Tears on their cheeks. He'd heard their sobbing.

His jaw hurt.

He faced the Plexiglas again, the rotors up to full speed.

And he was right. Nothing about this war ever ended. His heart shrank ... because ahead of him, diving out of the sun's glare, he saw the silhouette of a massive Soviet assault helicopter.

Massive didn't even describe it. A Soviet MIL MI-24. And even so far away, he recognized it because the silhouette made the MIL look like a monstrous hybrid of chopper and plane. A boxcar with rotors.

Jesus Christ, the sucker had wings.

And under the wings hung an arsenal. Weapons ... shit of every description. Cannons, rockets, missiles, their bulky silhouettes awesome.

And the damned thing streaked down with unbelievable grace.

Rambo popped the Huey off the ground, soaring toward the tree line. The assault chopper opened fire. The ground erupted to the right of the Huey, fountains of earth chasing it as it climbed.

But packed with men, the Huey barely cleared the trees in time, and Rambo veered hard to the left, trying to avoid the nosegun's aim. The prisoners jolted against each other. He peered up hurriedly and saw the Soviet chopper swing wide, once again aiming in his direction. He veered the opposite way, to the right now, as the tops of trees exploded.

The M-60 roared in back, Banks clutching its handles, returning fire.

The ground reeled, the horizon tilting, as Rambo nosed the Huey down, increasing speed. Tail high, it whipped above treetops, its nose radio antenna slashing upper foliage.

The assault chopper rolled on its side. Its wings providing stability, it managed an amazing sharp turn despite its bulk. It was easily twice the size of the Huey, with twice the power, and it loomed ever closer.

Frantically guiding the Huey, Rambo stared down at trees that rushed by, seemingly inches away, at a hundred and twenty miles an hour. The prisoners slammed against the bulkheads, the Huey plummeting and swerving.

Two rockets flashed by, exploding, fireballs rising from the jungle. As the Soviet gunship zoomed even closer, Rambo saw a zigzag opening in the trees and swooped down over a river. The trees on each side formed a narrow canyon, the walls of which overhung the river. The Soviet gunship was too big to come down here.

But maybe we shouldn't have, either, Rambo thought as the Huey flashed in and out of thick shadows. Ahead, branches curved so densely over the river that he had to fly under them, the Huey's landing skids throwing up spurts of muddy water.

Two more rockets flashed past. One exploded in a tree on the bank. The other hit the river. As Rambo passed the fireball, liquid spattered against the Huey's left side.

And the river kept turning, curving. Concentrating, almost with eerie second sight, Rambo anticipated, twisting, veering.

The forest exploded on the right, the shock wave punching the Huey. Whap! Shrapnel shattered the canopy. Jagged chunks of plastic and metal lanced Rambo's shoulder and chest, the pain so sickening that for a moment he feared his arm was broken. In back, a prisoner groaned as if hit.

The Huey shuddered. Its controls felt mushy. Its momentum slowed.

We're finished, Rambo thought. If another rocket explodes that close to us . . .

Never mind close. The Huey was chugging so lethargically now that the Soviet gunship would have no trouble aiming at it. Ten more seconds, maybe five, and . . .

Rambo eased back on the throttle, slowing the Huey even more, veered back and forth as if the chopper was out of control, and entered a long dark canopy of trees above the river. As soon as he reached its middle, he hovered in place.

"Banks! Look around back there! See if you can find a flare gun!"

"You want me to shoot at that thing with a stupid flare gun?"

"No! At the edge of the forest! Can you find one?"

"Yeah, I . . ."

"Do it!"

The flare exploded against the edge of the forest, smoke and flames rising.

Rambo tried to imagine what the Soviet pilot would think when the Huey didn't reappear on the other side of the canopy. The conclusion he hoped his enemy would reach was that the Huey had sustained serious damage, enough to force it down. The smoke and flames would add to his suspicion. The pilot would wait a few seconds, and when the Huey still didn't appear, he'd check the entrance to this tunnellike section of trees, and when he was sure of his conclusion, he'd hover, destroying the entire section with rockets.

Seven, Rambo counted.

He inched the Huey forward.

Six.

He paused again, yelling back, "Grab onto something!"

Five.

He increased the Huey's power.

Four.

He wiped blood and sweat from his eyes, his arm in agony.

Three.

His thumb was over the dragon's firing button.

Two.

One.

With the Huey held back at maximum power—he had the odd sense of a dragster spinning its wheels—he suddenly let it surge. Streaking forward from the canopy, he felt his stomach press against his spine. But at once it sank toward his bowels as he veered up sharply. Pivoting even more sharply, praying the chopper's controls would respond, he found himself alarmingly face to face with the Soviet gunship, so close that he saw the stupefied surprise on the pilot's face.

The last emotion the pilot would ever feel.

Rambo pressed the dragon's firing button.

Lightning. Thunder. The sky exploded.

— 20 —

"Lone Wolf to Wolf Den . . . Lone Wolf to Wolf Den . . . Do you read me? Over."

Murdock had ordered all radio transmissions switched to speakers instead of being channeled through the headset.

He tensed when he heard the voice.

Rambo's voice.

Exhausted, tortured.

"Answer him," Murdock said.

"We hear you, Lone Wolf," the technician said. "Come in."

"Prepare for . . ." Rambo sounded as if he inhaled sharply from pain. "Prepare for . . . emergency landing. Arriving with . . ." Another sharp breath, almost a groan. ". . . American POWs. Over."

The men who'd crowded around the console stared expectantly at Murdock, and when he didn't answer, they frowned. Some fidgeted angrily.

Murdock studied them, aware of their hostility. "Tell him"—Murdock thought about it—"tell him, 'Emergency landing confirmed. Good work, Lone Wolf. The party has already started.'"

Someone whooped, the impulse contagious, others joining in. They shouted, reminding Murdock of a high-school football team after winning a championship as they raced toward medical equipment, stretchers, fire extinguishers, foam for the landing pad . . .

The area quickly cleared.

Except for the radio technician, Ericson, and Doyle.

"Well, what the heck"—Murdock shrugged—"he's earned it, I suppose. Give him an escort."

"Fine with me. We'll have to wait, though"—Ericson peered at the radar screen—"till we see which sector he's using." He nodded. "Yeah, I see him now." And frowned. "But he's moving awful slow. In his place, I'd want to get my ass back here as quick as I could. No, something's wrong."

"All the more reason," Doyle said, "to get out there and give him an escort."

"American POWs," the technician said, shaking his head. "I might get patriotic again. I feel like I did in '73 when that other group came back."

"Yeah," Murdock said, "the war. It's over. But it doesn't end."

— 21 —

"Yeah, *Star Wars,*" Rambo said, talking to relieve his pain. "When you guys get back in the States, you'll want to see it six times. Some people saw it twenty."

The prisoners crowded closer behind him, spellbound.

"Skywalker?" Banks asked.

"Yeah," Rambo said, wincing, trying to keep the Huey steady, in such pain that he fought the urge to vomit. "And there's this guy with a black helmet and cape. Darth Vader. He's got this sword . . . except it's not a sword . . . it's a . . . There's the Mekong River ahead."

The prisoners no longer cared about *Star Wars*. They had something even more exciting to consider.

"And beyond it," Banks asked, "is that . . . ?"

"Thailand," Rambo said.

"And after that . . . ?"

"Home."

The word sent a hush through the Huey.

"Home," someone whispered. "All these years. Sometimes all that kept me sane was remembering . . ."

"Tastee-Freeze," someone said.

"Pepperoni pizza."

"Hot dogs. French fries."

"Beer and the Dodgers."

"My kid'll be sixteen years old now. He'll be able to drive a car."

"My wife. I wonder if she stayed . . ."

"What's it like over there?"

"Yeah, what's it like? In the world?"

Rambo hesitated.

"Well?" Banks asked. "What's the matter?"

"Nothing." Rambo couldn't bring himself to tell them. It would be too much. A sin. "Home? It's just the same," he lied. "The good old U.S. never changed."

"Come on, man. It must have."

"Sure. In a way, I guess. Ronald Reagan's president."

"Ronald . . . ? Wait a minute. You don't mean the movie actor."

"Yep." Despite his agony, Rambo had to chuckle. "'Death Valley Days' himself."

"Well, holy fuck."

"Yeah, I said that many times."

And Rambo couldn't bring himself to tell them that Vietnam was about to change its name to Nicaragua. Or that the sound of John Lennon's "Give Peace a Chance" had changed to the rattle of sabers.

And maybe that's why Luke Skywalker's light-sword was so popular. The clean depiction of war. If you had your hand cut off, you got a new one. In the movies. Yeah, John Wayne, Ronald Reagan, and the movies. No, he couldn't tell them about Nicaragua. It would be too much. Too god-damned much.

As the Mekong River grew larger ahead of him, he saw a speck in the sky beyond it.

— 22 —

Murdock sent the radio technician out of the hangar. "I'll handle this for you," he said. "You go ahead. Watch the sky for them." And when the technician was out of the hangar, he spoke to the microphone. "Pack Leader to Hammer. When the unidentified . . . repeat . . . unidentified helicopter has crossed the Mekong River into Thailand, shoot it down. Proceed to the crash site and fire your remaining rockets into the wreckage. No survivors. Repeat. No survivors. Is this understood, Hammer?"

Ericson's voice came puzzled through the crackling static. "Uh, sir . . . I'm experiencing a little hearing difficulty."

"What are you talking about? Over."

— 23 —

"Well, uh," Ericson said in the chopper, "my problem is—I've got something stuck in my ear."

What he had in his ear was the muzzle of Trautman's M-16.

In back, Doyle was sprawled unconscious. The tarpaulin, where Trautman had hidden between stacks of ammo cases, was thrown back. Trautman pressed the rifle harder against Ericson's ear and leaned ahead to switch off the radio. "Tell me, Ericson. Wouldn't you rather run a tourist shuttle service? In the south of France?"

Ahead, through the Plexiglas, he saw Rambo's Huey. And Rambo bleeding in pain at the controls.

But Rambo could see inside the Agusta's Plexiglas—Trautman was sure of it—could see Trautman pressing the rifle to Ericson's head.

And with the dignity of professionals—Trautman had trouble breathing—they nodded to each other.

Rambo, I love you.

— 24 —

Ignoring the foam on the landing pad, Rambo took the Huey straight inside the hangar, wavering, managing angrily to set it down. As medics and firefighters raced inside toward the chopper, he stepped from the open bay, clutching the M-60, his expression so fierce that everybody scattered back.

Except for one medic who peered inside the Huey and gasped at the blood that still sloshed.

Rambo's entire body was covered with it. Dripping, he left a trail as he walked.

Outside, the Agusta set down. As soldiers scurried to aim their M-16's at him, Rambo heard a voice bark from the Agusta's loudspeaker. The voice was Trautman's. "Put those weapons down! Repeat! Put down those weapons! That's an order from a very pissed-off colonel."

Rambo turned, peering out of the hangar toward the Agusta. Trautman stood at its open bay, aiming its machine gun toward the soldiers.

Trautman's eyes said everything.

In '68, in Saigon, they'd spent an afternoon in a bar together.

Trautman had said, "I've got two daughters. I'm glad they were daughters. I love them. I wouldn't want anything different, believe me. But . . . if I had a son, I'd want him . . . to be you."

And Rambo had replied. "My father drank and beat my mother. I was glad to be in the army. To get away from . . .

If I had a decent father . . . I'd want him . . . to be you."

And now exchanging glances, Rambo understood.

He had permission.

He swung his M-60 toward the computer banks, the radar, the radio, all the other consoles. He pulled the trigger, shuddered from the recoil, and blew the shit all to pieces, blasted it—as he had the prison camp—to hell. Consoles exploded. Computers disintegrated. Radar screens erupted.

It gave him great satisfaction.

But not enough. No way.

Swinging the machine gun, he focused on Murdock, who cringed against a wall. Stalking toward him, Rambo raged. His heart pounded. "You!" he shouted. *"You!* You're what's wrong! Because of maggots like you, I went over there the first time! And the second time! And both times, you betrayed me! You wouldn't let me win the first time! And you did your damnedest to keep me from winning the second time! But I won anyhow! *Didn't I?"* His neck muscles bulged so much he felt strangled.

"Hey," Murdock said and scrambled farther back, "don't confuse me with the guys that give the orders. I'm a middleman. I'm . . ."

"A tool," Rambo said, advancing with the machine gun. "A fucking tool. And what I'd like to do with your tool . . ."

"Now wait a second." Murdock skittered farther back. "You've got to—"

"What?"

"You've got to let me explain."

"Explain that guys like you—and the politicians who give you orders—would cause a lot less wars if you had to fight them?"

"Well, sure, I mean"—Murdock shook and huddled in a corner—"if you say so. Hey, whatever you say."

"What I say is this." Rambo raised the M-60, pointed it at Murdock, and pulled the trigger.

Click.

Murdock shit his pants.

The saturating yellow liquid streamed down his pant legs, gathering on the floor.

"More men are out there," Rambo said. "More prisoners ... You find them ... Or I'll find you ... And maybe, finally, this war will be over."

Rambo threw his machine gun onto the floor and turned to walk ...

... toward Trautman.

— 25 —

They paused and stared at each other's eyes.

"In the States, at the prison," his father said, "I asked you what you wanted. Remember what you answered?"

Rambo nodded. "I wanted someone to tell me ..."

"I'll say it back to you. 'You did good, John. You did good.' And mean it."

Rambo's throat constricted.

"And now?" Trautman asked.

"Don't know."

"You want some company?"

"Yes. I do. But ..." He almost vomited from what he'd been through, from the emotions he was feeling. "Not right now."

"I ... understand. I'd better let you go. You'll need those medics. But do you think ..."

Rambo waited.

"... it *is* now finally over?"

"After going through it a second time?"

"But this time you won. And for what it's worth..."

Rambo waited again.

"...for this, you'll get a second Medal of Honor. That's never happened before."

Rambo turned to the men being carried in stretchers. His heart went achingly out to them. "Give it to *them*."

"But what about you?"

"Me? Hey, don't you remember? What you taught me? The trick is... to survive."

"That's all?"

The question reminded him of a similar question that Co had asked him.

Co.

"That's all," Rambo said. "What else is there?"

In the background, Banks, on a stretcher, raised his thumb. "Hey, man, you did good!"

About the Author

In addition to his award-winning *First Blood*, David Morrell's other fiction includes *Testament, Last Reveille, The Totem, Blood Oath*, and the recent best seller, *The Brotherhood of the Rose*. He is the author of numerous short stories, an illustrated World Fantasy Award nominee, *The Hundred-Year Christmas*, and a critical book on John Barth. His fiction is characterized by strong vivid prose and intense compelling narrative.

He is a graduate of the National Outdoor Leadership School in Lander, Wyoming. He holds a Ph.D. in American literature from Pennsylvania State University and is at present a professor in the English department at the University of Iowa—"the mild-mannered professor with the bloody-minded visions," as one reviewer called him. Married, with two children, he lives in Iowa City. Aware of the difficulty that many non-Midwesterners have in differentiating Iowa from Ohio and Idaho, he thinks this is all to the good. "If they don't know where we are, they can't find us," he says. "If people knew how good we have it out here, they'd come in droves. Meat is cheap, the vegetables are sincere, and I've never had to worry about my children being mugged at the schoolyard. I can reach anywhere in town in fifteen minutes. I live in a house with a back yard that has forty trees and an animal population of squirrel, shrew, possum, mole, groundhog, raccoon, and on one fine misty morning, two deer. This becomes surprising if you realize that we live in the middle of town. Not to worry about these animals. Our Siberian husky keeps everything under control."